PLAGUE SHIP

& Other Tales

Dark Fancies & Strange Whimsies

Jonathan Natusch

OCCASIONALLY ERUDITE PUBLICATIONS

Gisborne, New Zealand

Occasionally Erudite Publications
P.O. Box 783
Gisborne
New Zealand 4040
www.jononatusch.wordpress.com

Publisher's Note: This is a work of fiction. Names, characters, places, and incidents are a product of the author's imagination. Locales and public names are sometimes used for atmospheric purposes. Any resemblance to actual people, living or dead, or to businesses, companies, events, institutions, or locales is completely coincidental.

Cover picture by Cocoparisienne via pixabay.com

Plague Ship & Other Tales : Dark Fancies & Strange Whimsies / Jonathan Natusch. -- 1st ed.
ISBN 978-0-473-41663-8

Also available in Epub form: ISBN 978-0-473-41664-5

Thanks to my oldest friend Ben Legg, who allowed the story I wrote for his birthday – Out of Phase – to be used for this collection. Ben, you've always believed I was creative. I hope I haven't let you down!

And a most profound thank you to my friend Nomes Lorimer for all the hours of time and effort reading everything, picking up my multiple errors, and providing feedback. No one could wish for a better editor! Any mistakes that remain are entirely my own fault...

One need not be a chamber to be haunted.

—EMILY DICKINSON

CONTENTS

FACTS & FEELINGS

I was at a low ebb when I met Jarred McKeen.

I'd had a girlfriend and a job, and now I had neither. In various movies I'd seen over the years, people in similar situations would disappear from life and go walking, and, while walking, would rediscover themselves or meet the woman of their dreams or discover some life-changing truth. It seemed worth a shot. It wasn't as if I was walking away from much. I'd moved in about a year ago to my now former-girlfriend's place, so her name was the only one on the rental agreement. Likewise, the internet, power and water bills were all in her name too.

So I walked.

I'd withdrawn a bit of cash - enough to make do for a short while without the use of bank cards, but not enough to make me live in endless fear of being mugged - and I had a small rucksack with some bare essentials. I was feeling minimalist and I liked it.

It took a while to make it out of town. I'd started walking late morning, and it was getting towards late afternoon before I left the suburbs behind and hit the open road. I have to say, the open road was somewhat of a misnomer. This wasn't the tree- and hedgerow-lined pilgrimage of latter-day tramps; this was a sterile, concrete-sided expressway. The planting that existed was equally sterile, planned by a roading engineer and designed for efficiency over beauty.

As walks went, it was beginning to lose its shine. My relief was therefore palpable when a truck pulled over and offered me a lift. If the driver was curious as to why I was out in the late-afternoon sun, making my way wearily along the side of a busy expressway, he didn't show it. We whiled away the hours till the next city with conversations about sports teams and movies. His daughter was in her first year at university, the first in the family to make it. He was a proud father. I offered no personal insights of my own.

When we reached the outskirts of the next city, he asked me where I wanted to be dropped. He had a cheap motel booked, one with a car park used to housing trucks. Although he tried not to be obvious, he was trying to tell me that this was where we parted company. One afternoon was enough; he wanted his solitude back for the next leg of his drive.

I leaped out next to an inexpensive-looking hotel. The sun had disappeared by now, and bright neon invited me in. First though, there were other important matters to attend to, namely the liquor store just up the road. As the truck departed with a cheery honk of its horn, I went on the hunt for bourbon. They concealed it in a plain brown paper bag, which I approved of: nondescript, just like myself.

Returning to the hotel entrance, liquor in hand and rucksack slung over my shoulder, I encountered Jarred McKeen for the first time. 'You!' he said, emerging out of nowhere and pointing at me in a jovial way. 'You look like the type of fellow who could use a drink!'

He seemed about my age - early- to mid-thirties - with a shock of blonde hair and a pair of trendy dark-rimmed glasses. He wore skinny jeans, and a green-checked shirt beneath a tweed jacket with leather patches on the elbows, the sort of jacket I'd always hated. Regardless of my thoughts *vis-a-vis* his taste in jackets, I gently waved my paper bag-encased bottle in the air. 'You're absolutely correct,' I replied.

He clicked his fingers happily. 'In my room I have vodka. And there's apparently ice in the freezer. A hotel room with a freezer! Luxury! You should accompany me, with whatever you're waving about, and we should drink a lot of it!'

'I thought I'd stay here, but I haven't yet checked in.'

'Check in can surely wait,' came the prompt response. 'This is *not* a busy hotel.'

He had a point. The 'vacancy' sign had most definitely been lit, and the foyer was most definitely empty.

'So follow me,' said McKeen, 'and let us drink!'

As I did as I was instructed, and followed him up the stairs - no elevator in this hotel - I had to admit to a feeling of uneasiness. No one here knew who I was, and no one who knew me knew where I was. If my new acquaintance was not what he seemed, then it would take quite some time, maybe never, for anyone to come looking for me. I shrugged of my disquiet. Hell, I'd gone walkabout of my own volition. Risks were to be taken.

Finding the correct door, my newly acquired drinking buddy struggled with the key, uttering a few choice words before jiggling the door open. 'This place is a shithole,' he declared. 'Thank god it's cheap.'

It did have glasses though, and a small fridge-freezer with ice, which was a darn sight better than *some* dives I'd stayed in, back in the day.

'So, what do you do?' I asked, as I poured my whisky and he poured his vodka, two ice cubes each.

My companion raised his glass above his head theatrically. He already seemed drunk. 'I, sir, am an associate professor. Can't you tell by my tweed jacket? Jarrod McKeen at your service.'

We took a slug from our glasses. 'So what do you teach?' I asked.

'English,' he replied, 'which is why I'm here.'

It turned out that there was an entire conference going on nearby, dedicated to William Shakespeare, the Bard Himself.

'Gods,' I shuddered. 'Wouldn't that get frighteningly dull? Day after day of people rattling on about Shakespeare?'

'Two days. Full days admittedly, but not as bad as you'd think, apparently. My first time this year, so I probably shouldn't speak too soon. Endless array of topics though - rethinking the meaning of individual plays; Shakespeare's contemporaries; his influence on modern film; origins of his own plays; his personal history; Shakespeare portrayed in modern literature…'

'So you're presenting?'

'Bingo!'

'And what's your subject of choice?'

'Shakespeare and the Templars.'

I was taken aback. 'You mean the Knights Templar who got massacred back in the 1300s, or the post-Templar organisations that muscled in on the vibe?' I'd read enough Dan Brown-esque nonsense to know the vague ropes. 'The Rosicruceans? The Freemasons?' McKeen shrugged. 'Meh. All of them.'

'You don't sound excited.'

'Well, it's all bullshit. But you've to get publicity.'

'So Shakespeare wasn't a Templar? Or a Rosicrucean or Freemason?'

'Nope, but I wrote a thesis linking him to them all, which got me a few news headlines. Which then got me a speaking slot at this gig, so that's the key thing. Plus, I'm hoping to expand and adapt the whole thing into a book, which might just get me into the big time circuit.'

'But it's all lies?'

Jarrod McKeen looked askance at me, then he threw back his vodka and poured himself another. 'Don't let facts and feelings get in the way of each other,' he said. 'I *could* write about Shakespeare on a strictly factual basis. That wouldn't excite anyone, and I wouldn't be an associate professor, and I wouldn't be speaking at this conference. *Or*,' he splayed one hand at me while taking a heavy slug of vodka with the other, 'or I could set forth a series of propositions that are exciting, that make you feel something.'

'But which are bollocks?'

'Utter bollocks. But, voila!' He waved an arm at his surroundings. 'I'm at a conference!' He plonked himself down in the room's sole armchair. I took the edge of the bed. 'Let me tell you about my philosophy,' he continued. 'Facts mean shit these days; feelings are everything. Take my thesis, for instance. I *could* deliver a well-researched explanation of some part of Shakespeare's life. It'd be worthy. And dull. And I wouldn't be making the occasional newspaper headline and getting invited to speak at conferences. No one cares about the facts. But! But if I spin a line of bollocks, it feels sexy. People embrace sexy. People want to rub themselves against sexy.'

'So what's the line you're spinning? How do you link Shakespeare to the Templars?'

McKeen contemplated his vodka as he chose his words. 'Well, the Knights Templar got themselves annihilated back in the 1300s, so it's more connecting Shakespeare with the Freemasons than the Templars. But if we're looking at the Templars, let's look at *Hamlet*. There's the two minor characters, Rosencrantz and Guildenstern. That's actually a code. At that time, Queen Lizzy the First had revived the age-old quest for the Holy Grail. Her personal astrologer - a fucked up dude called John Dee - had discovered a document explaining that two men named Rosenkreutz and Goldenstone possessed a *different* document that would decode the Bible and reveal the existence of the Grail.'

'Yeah?'

'Yeah. So, two theories: first, Shakespeare's giving a clue as to the names of these two men who hold the key to finding the Holy freakin' Grail; or secondly, he's encoding the names of two symbols which traditionally point to the burial place of the Grail - the Rosy Cross (Rosencrantz) and the Golden Stone (Guildenstern).' I raised my eyebrows in an unconvinced manner. 'Either way, it's esoteric. Esoteric is sexy.'

'And the connection to the Freemasons?'

It was a question I soon wished I hadn't asked. Apparently, the Freemasons hadn't actually existed at the time of Shakespeare, or if they had, it was the very beginnings of the modern order. Nonetheless, there had been *some* form of Guild of Masons since at least the 1200s, with their symbols of the stoneworker's trade - the square and the compass, which together form the well-known logo that adorns every modern Freemason's lodge.

And, of course, Shakespeare kept referencing Masonic symbols: the square, the rule and the apron. *Antony and Cleopatra*, Act Two, Scene Three: 'Read not my blemishes in the world's report; I have not kept my square, but that to come shall all be done by the rule.'

Or *Henry VI*, Act Two, Scene Three: 'Here, Robin, an I die, I give thee my apron.'

That was just the beginning. Almost anything seemed to be able to be read as a Masonic reference, if that were one's bent. And then there was a numeric Masonic code, the detail of which bored me to tears. An example: The number thirteen is apparently a powerful Kaballistic number. And on the cover page of the first edition of Shakespeare's sonnets, the supposed publication year of 1609 has a line all to itself. Zeroes in ciphers were generally treated as nulls, meaning 1609 was in fact 169. And 169 was thirteen squared!

In the midst of this utter bunkum, McKeen was throwing back his vodka like a champion. My cheap bourbon and I simply couldn't keep up. As his whirlwind tour of Shakespearean esotericism concluded, he brushed the whole topic aside with a simple, 'But it's all in the conference paper.' He pointed to a bound sheaf of papers sitting on the hotel floor. 'Anyone could turn up and present the damned thing. Even you!' He seemed suddenly tickled pink by the idea. 'Wouldn't that be bloody hilarious? You could present my paper!'

'I think they'd quickly recognise that I wasn't in fact you…'

His hilarity gave way to an abrupt dejectedness. 'Never met a single one of the fuckers. First conference. None of 'em'll know me from a bar of soap. Plus, I'm on at ten in the morning. Opening presentation of the day, so everyone'll be too busy nursing their hangovers to show up.' His expression brightened again, a new stop on his emotional roller coaster. 'Just the start though. Onwards and upwards! Soon I'll be the conference headline act!'

It wasn't much longer before I passed out. I'd spent too long walking in the hot sun, and the booze and lack of proper sustenance took its toll.

I awoke, still on the end of Jarred McKeen's bed. Shaking off the bourbon fog, I looked around for my host, ready to apologise. He was still in the chair that he'd inhabited the night before. His mouth was wide open, a long strand of white goo tracking its way down from his lips to his jacket. His eyes were open, and I sat up properly with a start, thinking he was staring directly at me. A closer inspection, after a brief embarrassed apology that yielded no response, confirmed that Jarred McKeen was now in fact deceased. There was a plastic bag lying at his feet, still containing a small amount of white powder. A dusting of powder covered his trouser legs and his upper lip. It didn't take a genius to work out what had happened.

I checked my watch and considered my options. It was not yet eight o'clock. I surveyed the room. McKeen's suitcase was lying open next to the bed. A brief rummage through, taking care not to mess anything up, confirmed that firstly, he had a one track mind when it came to his wardrobe (skinny jeans and tweed jackets abounded), and secondly, he had a significant drug problem. There were at least two more small plastic bags stuffed down the side of the suitcase, one packed full of cannabis buds, the other containing a small amount of white crystals. McKeen might have been the sort of fellow who would bring his own bath salts on vacation, but I somehow doubted it.

One thing was sure. When police and/or medical assistance was called for, there would be no doubt as to the cause of Jarred McKeen's death. Grabbing my now-empty bottle of hourbon, I placed it and my glass in my bag. Then, taking up the room's sole tea towel, I wiped down all the surfaces I could remember touching. McKeen would be remembered as a lonely academic, drinking vodka and snorting coke, alone in a cheap hotel room.

All I had to do now was walk out of the room, leave the building, and carry on my way. The maids would find McKeen's body in a few hours, and the cause of death would be swiftly established.

Meanwhile, I would be just another anonymous 'man on the street,' soon to be in a different city entirely, my drinking partner's fate an already distant memory.

Which made what I did next all the more surprising. On a whim, I reached into the suitcase and pulled out one of McKeen's back-up tweed jackets. Slipping it over my t-shirt, I thought I looked every inch the cool, young, wannabe professor. Then I picked up his conference speech notes. At some point before I had lurched into unconsciousness, McKeen had been waving them around, trying to convince me of some daft argument or other (forgetting he'd already espoused the intellectual dishonesty of his position) and they had remained on the floor by his chair.

Speech notes in hand, I made my exit. The conference venue was just a short walk away, and as I made my way there, I stopped off briefly to buy a pair of non-prescription McKeen-esque spectacles. I was rocking the look. The conference was being held at another down-at-heel hotel, of which this neighbourhood appeared to have a copious supply. A sign in the foyer, with 'THE BARD' printed in large capital letters, pointed me in the direction of the sole conference room. A large trestle table sat close to the doors, rows of plastic name badges lurking in grimly perfect alignment. This was a table that had been set up by a perfectionist. I stared at the lady behind the table, the presumed creator of the regimented badge line. She was an efficient-looking, early middle-aged brunette, sporting a fake smile that said, *Do not mess with my schedule.* 'Can I help you?' she asked.

'Jarred McKeen,' I said, introducing myself. 'Here to present my paper this morning.'

I extracted the speech notes from the inside of McKeen's jacket and waved them about.

'Oh,' she said, her lips tightening into a straight line as I found the correct name badge and knocked its neighbours out of position. 'You're kicking the morning off. Good for you.' She paused. 'You look different from the advertising material.'

'I was blonde then,' I explained, thinking quickly. 'New hair, new me.'

'Ah, that'd be it then. Well, head on in, grab a seat in the front, and I'll be in in a short while to introduce you.'

My conference presentation went surprisingly well. The crowd was small, barely a dozen onlookers who had crawled out of their respective fogs of booze to hear McKeen speak. I duly recited the pages of pre-prepared speech notes, and awaited the questions. There weren't many, just enough for those present to show they were still awake. Besides, my sparring with McKeen the previous night had given me a fairly good sense of how to answer.

I shook a few hands as I left the room, before disappearing out into the streets. A few blocks away, I dumped the bottle and glass from my rucksack into a nearby bin. Then, a few more blocks on, I found a small leafy park. I took off the jacket and sat down on a less-than-comfortable park bench, before leaving a short time later with the jacket still laying on the bench. I figured someone would take it away with them sooner rather than later. There was surely a homeless man lurking close by with a secret tweed fetish. A few blocks later, the spectacles met the same fate as the bottle and glass.

I still wasn't quite sure why I had done what I'd just done. A very simple police investigation would become rather more complicated. I could just imagine some bemused detective asking why someone would impersonate a recently deceased, drug-addled minor academic, purely to present an inane conference paper? All I knew was that it had felt good. I was a born-again subscriber to Jarred McKeen's philosophy of feelings over facts. My impersonation of him, in the face of what factually should be every good reason not to, could almost have been an homage to his memory.

If I analysed the facts, there was now every chance that the police would be looking for a fellow matching my description in relation to a very strange case of death and impersonation.

Facts be damned. Delivering a conference speech as a supposed Shakespearean expert had been a blast. As I walked on, my low ebb began to disappear. I had a feeling that life was going to be just grand.

AN INVESTIGATION INTO THE DEATH OF ALEX WILLIAMS

Alex Williams, aged fourteen, went missing at some point between departing the school bus at 3.30pm and the arrival home of his mother two hours later.

His mother, Sue, was the receptionist for a plastics company. It was the sort of company that didn't in fact create anything plastic-related. Instead, it simply imported plastic goods from China, India, Bangladesh, or wherever the cheapest factory-du-jour was located, before on-selling them to whichever other businesses required inexpensive, poorly-made plastic shit. Sue Williams' job was to redirect calls, since customers seldom physically troubled the reception desk. The phone would ring, she would ask who the caller was and who they wanted, before pressing a button to make it so. Then, at 5pm, she would depart, making the half hour car trip back home, in time to prepare dinner for young Alex.

It was a Wednesday when Alex went missing. Sue arrived home at the usual time and found the front door locked. This was normal. Alex, at fourteen years old, was legally old enough to be home alone, but that didn't mean that his mother wanted him leaving the front door open for all and sundry to wander through.

The *un*usual part was that Alex wasn't home. After calling his name several times and getting no answer, his mother made her way through the house, half-expecting at any moment to find the unthinkable. Instead, every room was empty. His mother checked the small backyard, calling his name loudly. There was no response. She dialled his cellphone. It rang and rang before going to voicemail. She called the parents of his friends, only to find he wasn't there either.

It was at that point she called police.

It began as a simple missing persons enquiry. Mother comes home. Child isn't there. Has child run away?

Things escalated quickly once a comprehensive search of the property was conducted. The house was empty, devoid of obvious clues. But there was a shed in the back garden, and the shed contained a pool of fresh, or relatively fresh, blood. Suddenly, abruptly, a sleepy missing persons case (which friend or relative would he be found with?) had become a murder enquiry.

***

Detective Sergeant Ian Bartlett found himself being dragged back on duty, despite having clocked off at 3.30pm, about the time that Alex Williams had gotten off the bus. A late-summer bug had swept through the station, leaving NCOs in short supply. 'What?' he asked, as the familiar number of the Watch House flashed up on his phone.

'Sorry sir - possible murder scene,' came the response. 'Wondering whether you could clock back on?'

Bartlett sighed. The current shift were already short-staffed, but that wasn't the issue. The shift sergeant, Rob Nikora, had a reputation for trying to duck out of serious crime. Putting your head into a murder investigation meant a high likelihood of being called as a witness, and Rob Nikora's involvement in any case that proceeded to trial dramatically increased the odds of an acquittal. He had once been known to ask a Crown prosecutor whether he could give evidence about what he thought the defendant had been thinking.

Bartlett sighed again. 'All right, on my way. What's the address?'

***

On arrival, Bartlett found that he didn't in fact have a great deal to do. Detective Constables Brendon 'Baz' Clifford and Fred 'Nuggett' Brown, who had been searching the property, had done a stellar job of securing the area, limiting the risk of contamination by outside elements. A forensic team was already in place, looking for possible prints or DNA. Was the blood in the shed that of Alex? It was a question that would take a day or two to answer, but the investigation had to proceed, at least initially, on the basis that it was.

The house was similar to most in its vicinity. It was part of a sprawling nineties property development, full of soulless, identical, brick and tile creations. The only upside was the developers' decision to avoid the plaster exteriors of so many similar developments that had resulted in entire suburbs of 'leaky homes' in the years that followed. Sue Williams' house was clean, far cleaner than most houses Bartlett could recall that also housed a teenager. The small back lawn was meticulously mown, with finely clipped edges. Ms Williams was evidently a woman with an almost pathological eye for detail.

Bartlett sat down with Alex's mother in the home's lounge, shifting uncomfortably on the faux-leather couch. The room seemed to encapsulate the blandness of suburban life. There was the big-screen TV as focal point, because everything of interest in life had to be beamed in, not created by the room's inhabitants. There were the fancy teacups on display, for every suburban housewife needed a teacup collection. Were they ever used? She probably barely drank tea. Nonetheless, standards had to be maintained. And the colours were all washed out; whites and greys, a palate that avoided even the merest hint of vibrancy. The lady of the house, she who had furnished the room, was herself entirely bland. She was the amorphous product of a dozen fashion magazines, her edges blurring as she tried to roll too many looks into one and ended up becoming nothing.

Bartlett hated these moments. There were tears, so many tears, as he attempted to piece together from her an account of Alex's usual movements. It was not a complicated picture. Alex would finish school at 3pm. At about 3.10pm, the bus would leave, with Alex safely aboard. At around 3.30pm, Alex would be dropped outside his home, the bus stop being a mere five metres from his front gate. He would wait at home for two hours until his mother arrived, and would then have his dinner cooked for him.

'Does he take part in any extra-curricular activities?' Bartlett asked. 'After-school sport? Chess club?'

'He's not very sporty,' explained Alex's mother, in between near-hysterical fits of crying. 'He's part of the chess club on Thursday lunchtimes though…'

It turned out that Alex was not an extra-curricular kind of kid. He took flute lessons on Mondays, from an elderly lady who lived five minutes walk away. Apart from that, all other notable activities occurred at school.

There were more tears.

Did Ms Williams have a partner? An ex-partner, perhaps? Someone who might want to hurt her by hurting her son? Apparently not. It had been years since she had seen anyone in any serious sense, and they had parted amicably.

The bouts of tears continued.

***

'Suspects?'

Back at the station, Bartlett still hadn't managed to escape. It was now after midnight, and he was due back on his usual shift at 6.30am. He'd sent a text message to his wife, apologising mightily, though she was used to such occurrences.

Detective Constable Maia Phillips was Barrett's sounding board. She was an enthusiastic, driven young officer, likely to make sergeant well before many who had graduated from police college at the same time. 'Well, first up has to be the father,' she said. 'Though why anyone would want to kidnap or kill a kid you don't even give a shit about, I don't know…'

'The mother's word only, at this stage.'

According to Alex's mother, the father had largely been out of the picture since just after the separation, when Alex had been four. He had no time for the child, and saw him once or twice a year, on special occasions like birthdays and Christmas, and even then only for a few hours.

'Imagine,' said Barrett, 'the dude gets fed up with his ex-wife giving him a day or so each year with his kid. He thinks, "Bugger the Family Court, I'll sort this out myself." So he tries to abduct Alex when mum's not home, but young Alex doesn't *want* to see his dad. And then there's blood.'

'Have they gone through the Family Court at all?'

'Blowed if I know. Should have asked.' Barrett made a note.

'Definitely wasn't the mother. Her work have assured us she didn't leave till her usual time. Stephens is following up with their statements,' she said, referring to another on duty constable. 'Neighbours?'

'That's a mission for tomorrow morning. The mother can't even name any of them. Close neighbourhood, huh? It's on the list for the next shift.'

Detective Constable Phillips stood up and made a few notes on the room's whiteboard. 'So,' she said, 'kid gets off the bus, nobody sees him again. Bus driver's the last guy to see the kid alive. And whoever else's on the bus.'

'I'll head over to the school tomorrow morning,' replied Barrett. He checked his watch. 'Today. Bugger.'

When the school buses began rolling in, Barrett was waiting. There were couches in the police social club lounge, and he'd grabbed a few hours sleep on one, intending to knock off early this shift if he could possibly swing it. The school's principal was standing with him, ready to point out the correct bus. He was a slight, nervous individual, worn down by a lifetime of needy or abusive parents, rebellious teachers and feral pupils.

'It's a shock. A horrible shock to everyone.'

'I'm sure it is,' murmured Barrett. Small-talk had never been his specialty.

The buses made their way in and out, disgorging their steaming cargo of students. Barrett stared at them in disgust. He had nieces and nephews, but wanted none of his own. These tiny tyrants were incomprehensible to him.

'That's the one,' said the principal, gesturing towards an incoming bus. 'Bert Haldane's the driver. Been driving for years.'

Thanking the principal, Barrett waited for the children to disembark, before wandering over and making his presence known. 'Mr Haldane?' he asked, stepping up into the bus.

'That's me. Bert's the name.'

Bert Haldane was a grizzled, shrivelled old man. He'd likely never been tall, but age had folded him in on himself, hunching him over the wheel. He had a shock of white hair that stuck out in all directions, yet despite looking as if he hadn't touched his hair since staggering out of bed, he was still clean-shaven. Barrett wondered whether the man was aping the 'artfully dishevelled' look of many young men in their twenties and thirties. He grinned inwardly.

'Mr Haldane, I'm Detective Sergeant Ian Barrett. I'm just needing to ask you a few questions about yesterday afternoon.'

'Ask away,' came the cheerful response.

'You were driving yesterday for the after-school run?'

'Just like every school day.'

'Do you know the names of any of the children you're driving?'

'Most of 'em. I try to ask their names and get to know 'em. Helps me know who gets on and off where. Nothing worse than a kid missing their stop! Causes no end of trouble. Why? Has one of 'em made a complaint against me?'

'Nothing like that, sir. Do you know Alex Williams?'

'Short, stocky kid? A bit shy? Yeah, I know him.'

'You remember him being on the bus yesterday afternoon?'

'Yep. Dropped him off, same as usual.'

'Who else gets off at that stop?'

'No one. There's about eight what get off just up the road, but he's the only one at his particular stop. Stop's right by his house. Right convenient. Mind you, kid might lose some of that weight if he had to walk a bit…'

Barrett smiled, despite himself, before etching his face back into a serious expression. 'The kid went missing yesterday. You remember anything odd when you dropped him off?'

'Odd?' Haldane pondered the question. 'Nope. Seemed all normal to me. Same as any other day. What do ya mean, he's missing? You saying he didn't make it home, 'cause I definitely dropped him off, and like I say, that's right by his house.'

'At this stage, we're still not certain what his movements were once he got off your bus. Do you remember seeing where he walked?'

'Not in the slightest. There was a line of cars coming up my tail, and I put my foot down to get back on the road before they caught me. Hate waiting for traffic. Puts me right behind schedule.'

There was not much more to be gleaned from Bert Haldane. Bartlett asked for a list of all the children who were still on the bus when Alex Williams departed it. It wasn't something Haldane could immediately supply. He'd need to stop the bus for a minute or two at the site of Alex's disappearance and take stock of who was still on board. He'd drop a list of names in to the station after the afternoon's bus run had ended. Bartlett rather hoped he would already be off shift and back home by that time. He told Haldane to simply leave the list at the front counter if he wasn't there.

Pity the poor soul or souls who had to interview all the children, just to check whether any of them had noticed something suspicious as the bus pulled away. It wouldn't be Bartlett's problem, for which he was profoundly thankful. There was a specialist child interview team. Children were dubious witnesses at the best of times - they needed specialist handling. He'd tee the team up to head in to the school the next day, once Haldane's list had been received.

From there, most of the day disappeared. There were other cases, other witnesses to chase up, other investigations that might be compromised if Barrett didn't keep juggling. By the time he made it back to the station, Maia Phillips had managed to contact Alex's father. At this stage, the guy seemed to have a cast iron alibi - he'd flown into the country just that morning after receiving a teary phone call from his ex-wife.

'Is he coming in to give us a swab?'

'Tomorrow morning,' affirmed Phillips.

A brief swab of the inside of the mouth was all it took these days to match DNA. Alex's mother had provided a swab the previous evening. Although the ESR technically needed just one parent's DNA to work out whether the blood stain had likely belonged to Alex, it was always more accurate to have two sets to cross-match against.

'He'll also be bringing in his passport and flight and accommodation records. I've left a message with the airline asking for confirmation he was on the flights he says he was, but they'll undoubtedly want a privacy waiver or warrant before they'll reply.'

Bartlett nodded. 'Are Baz and Nugget back?' The two Detective Constables were indeed back after an evening and morning of pounding the streets. 'All right, give 'em a yell. We'll meet up in my office in quarter of an hour.'

***

In the end, Bartlett's small office felt more than a little cramped with all four officers inside. However, there was a vacant meeting room just down the corridor, and an executive decision was made to transfer proceedings to the more capacious environment. The only downside was that none of the chairs were as comfortable as the one behind his own personal desk. 'So where are we at?' he asked of

Detective Constable Nugget, so nicknamed due to the shape of his head and its lack of hair.

'Bugger all of note to report from me and Baz, sir,' came the reply. 'We talked to all the immediate neighbours last night, once forensics had taken over the site. No one saw the kid get home, no one saw him leave. Almost all the neighbours were at work when the bus pulled up, and those that *were* at home weren't looking out their front windows at three-thirty.'

'What about back neighbours? We've got a pool of blood in the shed - no one heard anything?'

'Not a thing. We'll have to wait and see whether the search's picked anything up.'

Another team was currently going from backyard to backyard, checking for any sign of suspicious movement. Bartlett would touch base with them later.

'This morning,' continued Nugget, 'we went a bit wider afield - hit all possible exit streets. There's a few houses with security cameras, plus a dairy and a couple of other shops with CCTV. Took a look at any bit of footage showing the streets, but couldn't spot anything out of the ordinary.'

'Apart from that couple fucking,' interrupted Baz.

'True. At 4.56pm, there was a goth couple shagging outside the dairy. Brazen. Had to slap down my hard-on!'

'So,' said Bartlett, 'setting the public-sex-at-just-before-five aside, no one sees the kid leave the house or get taken. You got copies of any relevant CCTV?'

'Yup. Bunged 'em all in the evidence locker, but if we get a lead, I can drag them all out and review them. Might keep the goths for my personal collection...'

Bartlett stared up at the ceiling. 'So, let's think suspects. Who've we got? Can't be the mother - she was at work.'

'Can't be the father,' continued Phillips. 'He was out of the country.'

'Unless he paid someone. Guy never gets to see his kid; organises an abduction; makes sure he's out of the country when it all goes down.'

'Well, given the pool of blood, if it was an abduction, you'd have to say it was one that went wrong.'

'So what if it's a paid hit job then?' pondered Baz. 'Dude's blocked from his kid, so thinks, "If I can't have him, no one can have him." Mind you, damned odd to do it ten years after he and his ex separate…'

The most likely suspect, of course, was a complete stranger, someone who breaks in, thinking no one's home. A simple burglary gone badly awry.

'We're missing something,' muttered Bartlett. 'What's the kid doing in the shed?' Everyone considered the question. 'We've got a fourteen-year-old kid who doesn't seem to do much; who just goes home after school most days and waits for his mother to get home.'

'Drugs?'

'Secret girlfriend?'

'Okay,' decided Bartlett, 'Maia, head back to the house this arvo and have another look at the shed from that perspective. And do a full search of the kid's room. If he invited someone into the house - girlfriend, drug dealer, whatever - I want to know about it.'

'I can figure why he might get whacked by a drug dealer,' interjected Nugget. 'A girlfriend? Not so much. The main problem I have though is how whoever did this gets him out of the house? And why?'

Maia Phillips leaned forward intently. 'What do you mean, "And why?"'

'There's a struggle and there's blood. Why take the body, but not clean up the blood? You're more likely to get caught trying to dispose of the body.'

'That's assuming the kid's dead,' grunted Bartlett. 'What if there's a struggle, for whatever reason, but the kid just ends up injured? Someone might want to abduct an injured kid rather than just leave him to blab. Anyway, this isn't getting us far. Nugget, you're on DVD duty.' Nugget groaned. 'You're watching everything you gathered and noting every vehicle, make, model and number plate you can make out.'

'Shit!'

'Baz, start prepping search warrants. I want a warrant requiring the airline to confirm dad's flight details. Hopefully he'll just sign a waiver tomorrow, but I want a warrant ready to go. And I want a production order for his bank records. If he paid for an abduction-gone-wrong, I want to know where the funds went. Start with those and I'll get back to you.

'Maia, as discussed, you're on shed duty. Then liaise with forensics.'

***

As the meeting ended, the three Detective Constables made their exits, leaving Bartlett alone in the room. He wasn't someone who tended to get too emotionally involved in his work. Emotional involvement was an easy route to a comprehensive burnout. As a senior officer, you had to be there early in an investigation, just to protect your arse and make sure that the correct avenues were followed. He had now set things in train. It was time to wait and see what was unearthed.

Back in his office, another hour passed in a haze of phone calls and emails. His phone rang again for the umpteenth time. It was the front counter. Bert Haldane, the bus driver, was downstairs, if Bartlett wanted to see him. Bartlett cursed silently to himself. He just needed the list of names of the school kids still on the bus when Alex got off. Unfortunately, Haldane would now be well aware that Bartlett was in the building. 'I'll be down in a second,' he said sourly.

When he made it down to the front counter, Haldane shook his hand and proffered his list. 'Many thanks,' said Bartlett, 'we'll get a

21

team into the school tomorrow to interview everyone. I guess there's a chance someone saw something can help us.'

The bus driver folded himself over and bowed. 'One can only try to be of service, mate.'

Bartlett glowered at him. He didn't like it when people took the piss, and it had seemed suspiciously like Haldane's bow had been exactly that. 'One last thing,' he said.

'Anything, boss.'

'Just need a copy of your licence for the file. If you've got it on you, I'll quickly grab a photocopy.'

'My licence?'

'Just for completeness.'

He didn't need the licence. He could have run Haldane's name through the system regardless, but the bus driver's attitude had given him the shits. It would waste a few minutes of the man's day. Excellent. That it would also waste a few more minutes of *Bartlett's* day seemed an irrelevant consideration.

Haldane's licence in hand, Bartlett made his way backstage, behind the one way glass that allowed everyone to see what was happening out in the foyer. There was an available photocopier that Bartlett utilised, before he spotted one of the traffic division constables, Ramsey Elkson, sitting at a computer. 'Ram, mate, got time to run this licence?'

'Any time, sarge! I'm in the office - anything to break the boredom…'

Bartlett watched while Ram grabbed the licence and entered the information into the system. An error reading came up on the screen.

'Cool,' said Ram, and gave the licence back.

Bartlett took a few seconds to evaluate what had just happened. 'What do you mean, "Cool"? You got an error.'

Constable Elkson stared intently at his screen. 'Shit. Sorry, sir. Don't know what happened.' He grabbed the licence back and re-entered the information. 'There you go, sir,' he said, 'all good.'

Bartlett stared at the screen. Another error message was displayed. The licence information could not be found.

'Fuck's sake,' he swore. 'Give me the bloody seat!'

Elkson looked hurt. 'Sir? I'll need to log out if you want to run your own searches. If you've got other licences, just give me the details.'

'One search is all that's required, and you'll be watching. Give me your seat.'

Reluctantly, Elkson vacated his chair. Bartlett grabbed back the licence card and sat down. Staring at the card's details, he entered them into the computer system, before pressing 'search'. Nothing came up, just the same error screen. No such person. 'You see?' Bartlett asked.

'Oh,' said Elkson. 'Sorry, that's embarrassing. I've been working some odd shifts, sir.' The young constable could see an adverse notation arriving on his police record. 'Obviously a bit tired, sir. Hope you won't hold that against me.'

Bartlett looked down at the licence in his hand and felt the most profound sense of shock. There was no licence. He was holding a piece of blank card. He handed back the piece of card to Elkson. 'What do you see, constable?' he asked.

Elkson looked at him strangely, wondering the trick of the question. 'Um, well, it's the licence of a Mr Haldane, sir.'

'And my search result?'

Elkson looked back at the screen. He seemed to have abruptly forgotten the pair's previous exchange. 'Checks out, sir.'

'You what?'

'Um, licence seems fine, sir.'

Bartlett rose to his feet, staring at the blank piece of card in his hand. He turned, stepping away from Constable Elkson's chair and desk, staring back through the one way glass that separated him from the station's front desk. Bert Haldane was staring directly at him through the glass. It could have been coincidence - the bus driver simply staring into his reflection, unaware that Bartlett was opposite him on the other side of the mirror - but Bartlett didn't think so.

He strode towards the door that would take him back towards the public foyer, the useless piece of blank cardboard clutched in his hand. Through the glass, as he moved, Bartlett watched Haldane's eyes widen. The old man turned and ran, stopping briefly for the station's automatic doors to open. Bartlett, to get to the front lobby, had to open three doors, two of them with his swipe card, and cover a number of metres. By that time, Bert Haldane had well and truly managed to leave the building. Reaching the glass front doors, Bartlett stared up and down the street. Haldane was gone, remarkably quickly for such a seemingly old man.

Bartlett strode back into the building, swiping his ID to get back into the stairwell, and running to his second storey office to access his notes. He needed Haldane's details, and he'd stupidly left his police-issue notebook sitting on his desk. He cursed himself as he ran. The notebook contained everything he needed, and he'd have kicked the ass of any of his constables if they had left theirs upstairs, as he had just done. He burst into his office and fumbled back through the pages. There was Haldane's name, date of birth and address. Stuffing the notebook into his jacket pocket, he began running back down the stairs, calling over the radio for a squad car.

As luck would have it, a car was just pulling in to the station, back from taking statements relating to an assault case from the previous evening. There were two constables in the vehicle already, and Bartlett leapt into the back seat, barking out the address as he fastened his seat belt.

'What's the excitement, sir?' asked the constable in the front passenger eat.

Bartlett considered the question. A full explanation was beyond him. 'A guy did a runner from the station,' was his halfway-house response. 'I want to know why.'

'You sure he's heading where we're heading?'

'Haven't the foggiest. But this is the only address I've got.'

It was a short drive, less than ten minutes. The squad car pulled up in front of a rundown old house on an unremarkable suburban street composed mostly of old villas. Some had been renovated and painted; most hadn't. The house that Bartlett was interested in was a dilapidated bungalow, with a faded and cracked, decades-old paint job, and a rusting corrugated iron roof. A white-painted metal gate hung open, beckoning to a concrete path that led through an unkempt lawn.

Out the front of the house, parked on the street, was an immaculate old Holden Kingswood. It was the sort of vehicle Bartlett could imagine someone like Bert Haldane owning and loving. The old man may not have been house-proud, but if that was his vehicle parked out front, Bartlett could see where the attention had been lavished.

'So what's the plan?' asked the driver.

Bartlett directed the passenger-seat constable to cover the back door of the house, with the driver to make his way round the block and park out of sight. 'I'm not sure whether he's home. That might or might not be his vehicle. Don't want to frighten him if he turns up later while we're still here. Once you're parked, stay out of sight, and let me know if an old man suddenly shows up at the gate.'

Not knowing what to expect within the house, both Bartlett and the passenger-seat constable armed themselves with Glock pistols from the weapons safe in the squad car's boot. If he was walking straight into an ambush, Bartlett wanted rather more firepower than his standard-issue taser.

He made his way through the gate and down the path. There was a minor curve halfway, and the grass in between had been trodden down by someone unwilling to follow the path when a shortcut beckoned. He knocked at the front door, not expecting a response. The seconds passed and the house remained quiet. He tried the door knob. It turned, and the door swung open.

Bartlett entered carefully. He didn't understand what had happened back at the station - Constable Elkson's bizarre behaviour, and the licence that wasn't. Now that he was here, hunting down an old man who had fled the station, he was beginning to doubt his own sanity. Licences were licences, and licence checks checked out.

The hallway was empty, not just of a human presence - Bartlett excluded - but also of furniture and pictures. The Detective had expected at least the obligatory hall table, with phone and knickknacks gathering dust. He kept walking, ears pricked for the slightest sound. He was aware that he was now in dubious legal territory, entering a house without a warrant. His suspicion that Haldane had committed a crime hinged purely on the strange events back at the station, which he would not have wanted to describe to any of his colleagues, let alone a judge, lest they think him insane.

The hallway ended, separating off into either a dilapidated lounge to the right or a further corridor to the left. The lounge was a characterless desert, containing nothing but a large television and a single lazi-boy armchair. Just as with the hallway, there was no decoration, no personality. Bartlett began to move slowly down the corridor, still listening intently, when the sound of cutlery and crockery erupted from the doorway up ahead on his right. For the first time in some years, Detective Sergeant Bartlett unholstered a firearm. Holding the pistol out in front of him, he stepped forward and swung right.

Bert Haldane sat at a small plastic kitchen table, a knife and fork in his hands. In front of him sat a hunk of meat on a plate. Haldane was staring at him, but it wasn't the Haldane that Bartlett remembered. *This* Haldane had a sharp, pointed face, with strange, elongated ears. His cheekbones were eerie, inhuman, and when he smiled in greeting, his teeth were pointed, animal. 'I see my glamour doesn't work on you anymore. You're stronger of mind than the rest.'

Bartlett stared at him, now truly doubting his own sanity. 'What *are* you?'

The creature that was Haldane didn't just smile. It positively grinned, exposing every one of the razor sharp teeth that inhabited its mouth. 'Well,' it chuckled, 'for the most part, I'm one of you. Your friendly bus driver, don't you know?'

'But?'

'But I'm also something… other. And most of your flimsy species cannot comprehend that anything different walks among them. I project how I want them to see me, and that's what they see. I hand them a card, and they see a licence. They process my supposed details into their precious computers, and then they convince themselves to see what I want them to see. But *you*…,' the creature that was Haldane paused, moving its lower jaw in contemplative circles, 'you're rather stronger. You see the world just as it is.'

'So what happened? With the kid.'

'Oh, I noted the lack of adult attendance at the child's house. I'd pop back after my school run and keep watch.'

'*So what happened?*' Bartlett asked again, grimly.

'Well, I leapt a few fences, through properties where my research had shown that no one would likely be home, and I made my way into his back yard. Didn't even need to enter the house!' The creature that was Haldane chuckled. 'The little horn-dog was masturbating in the back shed. So exciting. And so I took him and feasted. And carried the remains away for later.'

'The remains? You left no blood traces or exit marks.'

'I came prepared. I *love* plastic wrap. Mankind's greatest achievement. As for exit marks, my kind are stronger than you'd give us credit for. Your high fences? Like nothing to me.'

'So you took the body. What did you do with it?'

The creature that was Haldane smiled a smile that chilled Bartlett's blood. It sawed off a chunk of the meat on its plate and held it, gently oozing, in the air. 'The second greatest of your species' inventions is the refrigerator. When I first journeyed to your country, the refrigerator was still a mad vision of the future! We had to salt our meat if we wanted to savour it over time…'

Bartlett shook his head in disbelief. What he was hearing was impossible, but then what he was seeing, and had seen, was impossible too. 'How many people have you killed?'

The creature that was Haldane licked its lips. 'Too many to even contemplate. But I've always had a soft spot for the children. It's why I took up the school bus gig. To scope out the vulnerable. A child here and there? Nobody looks twice at the bus driver.'

'How many kids?' It was a question Bartlett felt he had to ask.

'Oh, I've been driving school buses for a lot of years in a lot of places. It's just another number I don't keep track of. But it's been nice talking to you.'

And with that, the creature that was Haldane launched itself across the room, casting its knife and fork aside as it moved. Bartlett lurched backwards, crashing to the floor as the creature cannoned into him. His left hand closed around its throat as it came for him. Spiked teeth gnashed the air in front of him, scant inches from his face. The creature had been right - it *was* strong.

Thankfully, his right hand was between him and his foe. He still held the police-issue pistol. Other officers might already have pulled the trigger, taking the creature in mid-flight, but it had been a long time since Bartlett had been forced to use a firearm in earnest. He didn't have the reflexes for it that many of his younger officers did. Nonetheless, his finger was on the trigger, and he squeezed it tight. The creature above him jerked. He fired again, and the pressure above him subsided, the body rolling away to the side.

Bartlett got to his feet, panting heavily, his eyes wide. Next to where he had been lying, the creature that was Haldane lay in a growing slick of ichor. 'You've lasted this long because no one's seen you before for what you are and shot you.'

The creature writhed, spitting obscenities skyward. Bartlett took pity on it, putting a third and final bullet through its gaping, agonised mouth. All movement ceased. The Detective breathed a long sigh of relief, and as he did so, the whole carcass began to melt away, as if it had never been. Blood boiled, and flesh melted down to sinew and bone, which were abruptly nothing but more blood, which boiled away. For a brief moment, a dank film coated a section of the floorboards, but even that, shortly, was gone. All that remained was a bullet hole in the floor where a flesh-covered face had once lain.

***

29

There was an independent investigation, as there was every time a police officer drew a sidearm and opened fire. Bartlett had fired three shots, but there was no body. The members of the investigating panel seemed to readily accept the Detective Sergeant's evidence that he had been spooked by, and then had shot at, an animal. They weren't overly inclined to look too closely at Bartlett's firearms practices when it was revealed that most of Alex Williams' remains were ensconced in the refrigerator of one Bert Haldane, former school bus driver. Further, part of Master Williams' remains were on the plate in the kitchen, presumably being devoured by the animal at which Detective Sergeant Bartlett had loosed three rounds.

The murder of Alex Williams remained an open file. Bert Haldane was never found.

And Detective Sergeant Bartlett was left to nurse a story he could never tell, a story that eventually, decades later, he wasn't even sure he believed himself.

PLAGUE SHIP

Day Four

Patient Zero was dead. He had suffered massive, total, catastrophic organ failure. It wasn't simply a matter of a single organ - the liver, for instance - giving up the ghost. All of his major organs had been going into shut-down. Their cellular structure had been collapsing. In essence, his insides had been liquefying.

Cause and effect. Organ collapse was the effect; the cause remained a mystery. It was viral - that seemed certain. And it was highly infectious. But that was where the known quantities ended. Whatever had killed him had never featured in any medical textbook.

The room was bleak. White walls, white ceiling. Light-blue industrial-looking vinyl. Stainless steel fixtures - a sink and several shelving systems. This was a room ideally suited to being washed down and sanitised. In the centre sat a hospital bed. Cords ran from the bed to the nearest wall, taped to the floor to prevent those walking around the bed from tripping. Various stands held electronic equipment and bags of fluids, now rendered obsolete by the patient's passing.

And on the bed lay the erstwhile Patient Zero. He was young, just twenty-four years old. Shoulder-length black hair. He lay enshrouded by a hospital gown, the white hospital sheet pulled down so that it covered just his feet.

The cadaver that had once been Patient Zero, aka Chris Bretzner, was surrounded by five individuals in full biohazard suits. Not a centimetre of skin showed. The figure who stood at the very end of the bed spoke. 'Doctor Morrell is exhibiting the same symptoms as Bretzner did yesterday, as are Mr Symes and Mr Baker. They all interacted with Mr Bretzner two days ago, and their symptoms appear to be just a day behind those of Mr Bretzner. Whatever they have, it seems to be lethal within three days. God help us.'

Day One

Chris Bretzner was at Ronny's Basement for one of his favourite musical acts. They were a heavy, alt-rock act, yet to attract much of a following. The venue was small, but it was still far from full. Just a few dozen hardcore supporters were there, having paid their $10 cover charge. The crowd may have been sparse, but its energy was legion. They pressed forward against the stage, screaming along to the words that belonged to them and them alone. Chris had only found out they were playing at the last minute. He'd tried his best to drag a few friends along at short notice, but his friends lacked the fervour. Undaunted, Chris had sallied forth alone.

With no accomplices to share in his vibe, he found that his attention kept getting caught by a particular girl. She stood out amongst the assembled crowd for two reasons. First, was her choice of clothing. Amidst a sea of black, she wore a floating, tie-died skirt, reminiscent of the hippy festivals of yesteryear. Her midriff was on display below a cut-off, white top with puffed sleeves. When she held up her arms, the top was barely long enough to cover the base of her breasts. Secondly, there was her dancing. She moved in a way that bore no resemblance to the music: floating, wafting movements, all fingers and arms, when the bruising rhythms of the music demanded jerking syncopation. She appeared to be dancing to a soundtrack from a very different reality.

Chris watched as she idly stroked the back of a short-haired, black t-shirted man, who barely seemed to notice. He felt unaccountably jealous.

The girl moved on, drifting through the crowd as if it wasn't there, and then suddenly she was in front of him. She had her back to him, as if for the first time she was actually focussing on the band on stage, but she stepped backward slightly, somehow pressing herself against Chris without stumbling. She moved her hips, and Chris moved with her. He placed his hands on her hips and held them there, wondering whether to move them, and if so, where to. The decision was suddenly no longer his to make. The girl placed her hands over his and moved them around her so that they encircled her midriff. Then she took his right hand and began to run it higher, up beneath her top, until it rested on her right breast. She wasn't wearing a bra, and his hand began to twitch.

She turned her head towards Chris, as he pulled her tightly against himself. 'You wanna fuck?' she asked, just loud enough for him to hear, as the music pounded away in front of them. It was a silly question. Chris was already rock hard behind her, pressing himself eagerly against the curve of her arse and the small of her back. He'd been assuming that she'd either lead him outside or into the bathrooms, but she merely turned, ground herself against him, and asked, 'Right now?'

There was nothing sensual about fucking on a dance floor. She hitched up her skirt, while he, scanning the room awkwardly, teased out his cock. The thrusting was ungainly, but it got the job done. Around him, his fellow music-heads pointedly ignored him. It was difficult not to notice what was occurring, but, equally, it was bad form to stare at the rutting of others.

Then, just like that, she was gone. Chris hadn't yet finished, but there she was, pulling away, dropping her skirt, and walking towards the door. He looked down, fumbling awkwardly with his erection, trying to hide it in his jeans. By the time he was done, the girl had departed, out the door and away into the world. Chris remained, but

Ronny's Basement was now a sea of humiliation. He'd just fucked someone in public and then had them walk out before he'd even managed to cum. He'd been left with his dick out on the dance floor. He haphazardly nodded his head in time with the music until the song that was playing ended. Then he too left.

Day Three

Every hospital had protocols in place in case of epidemic. Whole wings or floors would be quarantined, all staff or patients suspected of contact with those infected shuttered within. Those were now in action in New York's Bellevue Hospital Center, as indeed they were across a number of the city's hospitals. The fear was that it was already too late.

Chris Bretzner had awoken two days ago feeling wretched. He was running a temperature, and the concept of food was anathema. He had popped a painkiller or two, phoned in sick to his work as a motorcycle courier, and returned to bed. As the morning had progressed, the fever had gotten worse, and he'd thrown up and noticed what looked suspiciously like blood. His local doctor's clinic was just two blocks away, easily walkable, but he'd called a cab. His legs were rubber. It had been a nearly three quarters of an hour wait at the clinic, and the doctor - a fresh-faced, newly qualified fellow, who introduced himself as Doctor Morrell - had merely nodded sporadically at Chris, before prescribing him some antibiotics. At the reception desk, as he'd pulled out some cash to pay, Chris had collapsed and been rushed to hospital.

It had been an embarrassment for Doctor Morrell. More than an embarrassment. He'd spent the afternoon and evening worrying about medical malpractice suits. Then, the next morning, he'd collapsed as he'd entered the clinic. He'd been overworked, not wanting to let the side down by admitting he was feeling like shit. Now he was in hospital, likely to die tomorrow.

Tying the Bretzner and Morrell cases together was almost instantaneous. A patient collapses, and within a day the doctor who had seen him goes down in a screaming heap too. Chances were not being taken. And all the while, other cases were coming in. A cab driver. A liquor store employee. A security guard. A guy who worked in a bulk barn. The cases kept coming.

The Bretzner-Morrell connection was enough to activate the protocols. At that stage, Chris Bretzner was still lucid and able to provide a description of his movements and actions in the days leading up to his hospitalisation.

***

There was a whiteboard, filled with names and descriptors. Arrows attempted to connect them up, explanatory notes added where available and applicable. In the centre of the whiteboard, the only name without an arrow leading to it, was 'Chris Bretzner'.

***

'Patient Zero. Every case this hospital has tracks back to him. He's the centre of the contagion.

The speaker was a tall, slim, African-American woman in her mid-forties, the sole woman and the sole black person in a sea of white men. She wore her hair in an unapologetic affro.

'So where did it come from then, Doctor Jewell?' asked a besuited, bespectacled fellow who appeared to be more bureaucrat than medical professional. 'These things surely don't appear out of nowhere?'

Doctor Jewell did her best to suppress a sigh and eye roll. 'That's obviously one of the major investigations that're currently underway.''

'But what do you know?'

'Well, in the time that our Patient Zero, Mr Bretzner, was here in the hospital and conscious, we tried to get as much info as possible about his movements. We've already had Customs and Border Protection confirm that he's never left the country, at least not legally. We've asked you lot in the Feds to check whether there're any records of him crossing state lines in any sort of strange way.' She gave the bureaucrat a most direct look. 'I would have thought this was something you'd already have been aware of.'

She received a sour look in response. 'Yes, I'm well aware of what my colleagues are investigating. I'm asking you about the *medical* side of things.'

Doctor Jewell continued as if she hadn't heard him. 'In terms of his day-to-day movements in the build up to his hospitalisation, the only behaviour that would cause any heads to turn is his engaging in sexual congress with a young lady at a concert. On the dance floor, I believe.'

The bureaucrat nodded, making an approving sort of face that Doctor Jewell found vaguely repellent. 'So he's fucked some girl in a club or whatever. Is he really our Patient Zero? What about her?'

'As I say, all the infectious cases our hospitals are seeing can be traced back to interaction with Bretzner. If this girl were our Patient Zero, we'd be expecting to see outbreak clusters relating solely to her movements. We're not seeing that. As to the medical side? How the hell he picked it up? That's an utter mystery. We've got a lot of people working around the clock to try and get a handle on what exactly we're facing and where it could have come from.'

'Okay.' The bureaucrat nodded, before nodding a little more as if killing time while he tried to think what he should say next. 'Hey, look,' he finally spluttered, seeming suddenly a lot more human, 'I'm not trying to be a dick about this. This thing's scaring the shit out of us. It comes out of the blue just a day ago, a single case, and we're already seeing dozens of hospitalisations. Nothing fucks people up that quickly.'

Doctor Jewell gave him a sympathetic look. 'It's evidently a highly infectious, fast-acting virus. It scares the shit out of me too. We've got our ads running, although I'd like to see a helluva lot more done in a practical sense.' The ads were state-wide, telling anyone who was suffering flu-like symptoms to immediately quarantine themselves in their home and to call emergency services. A team, in full biohazard suits, would be dispatched to check them out. Resources were already running thin. 'As to the girl, Patient Zero's sexual partner? I understand the city cops are trying to trace her movements and whereabouts, just to make sure she's okay.'

Day Five

Patient Zero was dead, and the new soon-to-be-casualties were mounting up fast. Doctor Morrell and three others had died that morning. All but one of Morrell's colleagues were now hospitalised, not expected to survive more than the next day or two. In the hospital itself, there were many who had been in contact with the infected patients before the quarantine protocols had been implemented. A significant proportion were hospitalised themselves.

In New York, Doctor Maggie Jewell was in another meeting. It was by video-link. Quarantine zones - both within hospitals and within state buildings to ensure the safety of city and state officials - were in place all over New York, making physical meetings difficult, if not impossible, in many circumstances. This particular meeting was just about to take a strange turn. The speaker was a young, slim girl in her mid-twenties, who had been tasked with collating information on all known affected patients. She was sitting at a paper-strewn desk, staring uncomfortably down the barrel of the webcam. 'They're all male,' she said.

Doctor Jewell frowned. 'What, city-wide? All male? That can't be right.'

'It is. Every single patient is male.'

The doctor paused, choosing her words carefully. 'This is going to sound horribly patronising, but are you sure you haven't had a spreadsheet filter error?'

'Not patronising at all. A pretty valid question really. And no, I've checked a fair few times. No error. They're all men. Every single infected patient.'

Later that day, the team that Doctor Jewell headed received a Police Department report regarding the movements of the girl from Ronny's Basement. She'd been caught on three different CCTV cameras before she caught a cab. The cab took her to JFK airport, where she'd caught a flight to Boston. Her name was Joanne Aldercroft. She apparently lived in Boston, although Boston PD had been unable to locate her at her home. Once she had landed and left the airport, she'd disappeared into the maze.

***

That evening, reports started coming through of infections in Boston. And San Francisco. And Los Angeles. And Dallas. And Miami. And Washington DC.

Doctor Jewell sat at her desk in her lonely office in a quarantined hospital in a medically besieged city, and stared in horror at the notifications she was receiving. She stood, crossed to her office door and locked it, checking once to make sure her action had been successful. Then, office secured, she cried. She'd extrapolated infection rates, and the current one hundred per cent mortality rate. Anyone with that knowledge would have cried, but they were still tears she wanted to cry alone. Knowledge without a solution could be a terrible thing.

Then she cast her mind back to the girl in the club, Joanne Aldercroft of Boston. And she began to wonder.

Day Thirty-six

The bitch had killed him.

He lay there, alone in his double bed, writhing and sweating. He knew enough to be well aware that he was now a dead man. He had a day or two left, that was all.

Like most of his sex who were still alive, he had voluntarily quarantined himself in his house the moment the panic had unfolded. He was luckier than many. He lived on the very outskirts of Green Bay, Wisconsin. It was the point where the city became rural, and he had been sitting on about ten acres of productive farmland, which had been increasing nicely in value, at least until all of this shit had gone down. By rights, he had been easily placed to be one of the survivors. Never one to put all of his eggs in a single basket, he farmed a number of different vegetable crops. He even had his own fuel tank, which would keep his tractors running for months before he had to consider raiding fuel from others. He could have survived almost indefinitely.

Then he'd fucked it all up. There'd been a girl in one of his fields. She'd had a basket - not a small basket either - and had been loading it with his freshly grown produce. From her perspective, the field had probably looked like an untended mess. After all, he'd been concentrating on staying indoors, away from human sources of contamination, rather than on making sure his lines of vegetables were free of weeds.

The problem was that he'd also spent more than a month masturbating. Before everything imploded, there'd been a girl who'd come round occasionally and put him out of his misery for a relatively affordable rate. She'd called herself Anna, although he had no idea whether that was her real name. She didn't come around any more. So then he'd seen the girl in the field. She was alone and she didn't look that strong. And she was pretty. She had short, strawberry-blonde hair that he could just see protruding from beneath the wide-brimmed hat that was protecting her from the sun. He'd always been a sucker for blondes. "Anna" had been blonde.

He'd watched her closely for a few minutes. She was wearing comfortable-looking trousers and a brown long-sleeved blouse, ideal for a foraging mission. She was taking her time, obviously taking stock of what crops were in the field. Every so often she would look around nervously, taking special note of the house, but he was well concealed behind his window and she never noticed him. It had taken him a while to notice her weapon, the handgun protruding from the edge of her basket. She'd come prepared.

He had left the window and fetched his shotgun and a knife. The knife was a US Army replica, sharp as all hell. His brother had given it to him back in the day. Looking at it nestling smoothly in his hand, he had wondered for the umpteenth time whether his brother was now even still alive.

He had quietly opened the front door, shotgun in hand, and ordered her to freeze. She'd frozen. He'd told her to put down the basket, taking very special care not to go for her gun, and to step several metres to the left. She'd complied. She also compile when he'd ordered her to pull down her trousers. As he'd got his end away, he'd kept the knife in his right hand and close to her body, a sharp reminder of the need for her continued obedience. When he'd finished, he had let her take her basket and the produce she had already collected, though he kept her handgun. He'd almost felt like a gentleman, letting her keep her ill-gotten gains.

Now though, a day and a half later, he was bedridden, fighting an ache that had enveloped his entire body. He knew what was coming. He was a dead man. Looking back, he realised that he had misread the girl's eyes. As he had done what he had done, he had tried to avoid her look of hatred. Seeing her eyes again in his mind, he realised that although the hatred had indeed been present, there had also been a vicious triumphalism. She had known she was infected, known she was killing him.

He had heard that it wasn't pleasant, not that the process of dying was ever likely to be particularly nice. He was going to die alone and, for the time that he was conscious, he would be in a great deal of pain. From the table beside his bed, he took hold of the girl's pistol. He was glad to have kept it. It would be easier than the shotgun or knife.

Day Seven

The same team was assembled, Doctor Jewell again as chair. Frankly, it would have been a surprise if any member of the team *hadn't* been there. They were all holed up in the same wing of the same building, which was under stricter than strict quarantine measures. No entry, no exit. Information came in thick and fast via a multitude of screens - packages of data and patient records, live video calls with updates, emails with back and forth queries.

The United States of America had gone into full panic stations. What had once, just a few days ago, been a city-wide problem had now escalated to a nation-wide meltdown. Infectious cases were being reported on all coasts. Seattle and L.A., Houston and Miami, Boston, Philadelphia and D.C. - they'd all followed New York with their own spreads of infection. Internet, TV and radio ads had been booked across the country. Showing symptoms? Stay home. Call 911.

The bureaucrat was giving an update. He was looking different these days. He'd stopped shaving, for a start. It may have been official agency policy to maintain a smooth chin, but ensuring clean facial lines now seemed the least of his worries. He had dark rings under his eyes, though this was a characteristic shared by every person in the room. No one was sleeping right these days. 'Okay, we found and then lost Joanne Aldercroft. She was stopped trying to leave Boston by car last night - one of the travel advisory checkpoints. She was the passenger. The guard recognised her. Then she shot him in the face.'

'She got away after shooting a guard in the face?' someone asked.

'Most of those checkpoints are just one or two man operations.'

'Person,' interrupted Jewell.

'Sorry?'

'One or two *person* operations.'

The bureaucrat grimaced. 'Whoops. Anyway, they're all hazard suited up. There're only so many suits to go round. And there's only so many *people* full stop to man the checkpoints. Am I allowed to say "*man* the checkpoints?"'

'I'll let it slide.'

An eye roll. 'There's no authority yet to turn anyone back if they really wanna leave, so there's no real point in having too many personnel on any one checkpoint. This checkpoint? One guy. He's dead, and Aldercroft is long gone.'

Doctor Jewell stared at him intently. 'How do you know he recognised her?'

'Body cam with microphone. They're basic police issue, but some have them, some don't. This guy was wearing one.'

'Why would she shoot? What did he say to her?'

'It was fairly innocuous. "Hey, you're Joanne Aldercroft, aren't you? We've been looking for you." Then she blows him away.'

'So she's gone.'

'Yep. Doubt we'll be picking her up on our radar any time soon. Anyway, Doctor, I hear that Miss Aldercroft's whereabouts is the very last thing we should be worried about.'

Doctor Jewell nodded slowly, her lips drawn together, holding her breath. 'Yeah,' she said, slowly exhaling. 'So. The fact that everyone who's fallen sick and/or died has been male? We've had testing done of a bunch of women who've been in contact with infected men. The testing is coming back with damn near uniform results. They're all infected, there's just no ill effects.'

Another member of the committee - an elderly man in a bow tie - spoke up. 'So, let's imagine you're infected, Doctor. You walk into this room. We're a collection of men. You're saying that within three or four days we're all dead, and you wouldn't have even felt like you had a cold?'

'That's what it looks like.'

'My giddy aunt. So we've been telling people to quarantine themselves the moment they feel any adverse symptoms, yet half of those who are infected have been walking around feeling no symptoms whatsoever? And have been spreading whatever this is to everyone they meet?'

'It would appear so.'

He slumped in his seat, his jowls shaking. 'We're done for. We can't stop this.'

Day One Hundred

The street was deserted. He remembered the way it had once pulsed with life, score upon score of people bustling back and forth. Street vendors, cafe tables and waiters, phone-bound pedestrians: they had all vanished in a shockingly profound upheaval. The high-rise buildings still stared down, but they were now self-imposed prison units, or morgues.

A dog loitered in the centre of the street, maybe half a football field's length ahead of him. It looked like a labrador, although from this distance he couldn't be sure. Once a pet, now a scavenger. He couldn't recall ever seeing big dogs like that on the streets, back when the streets were populated. Small, pointless dogs, yes, the one's more suited to handbags than real life. He wondered where the maybe-labrador had come from.

He had a name, but that seemed irrelevant these days. A name required a community. He walked past a bakery. The windows were smashed, presumably to get at whatever stocks of flour and other ingredients they had held. He'd read once that the average modern city held only enough food to feed its populace for two days. Supply lines were in constant momentum, refuelling any city with an endless chain of shipping containers, track and trailers, and railway carriages. Ban all movement in or out of a city for any extended period of time? Watch the chaos unfold.

He was a survivalist. His native city had been Chicago, but he also had a hut up in Wisconsin, in the forests of the Northern Highlands. When the coastal cities went into shut-down, and before the outbreaks, panic and controls arrived in Chicago, he'd hit the road north. He'd kept the hut well supplied. It had a concealed cellar, loaded with weapons, ammunition and non-perishable goods, more than enough to keep a man alive while civilisation crumbled around him. The hunting was good too. The forest around was well-populated with white-tailed deer, and he'd kept himself in relative comfort for several months, monitoring the disintegration of society through his radio.

He had a generator, and a fair few large jerry cans full of fuel, but although he was sparing with its use he'd been worried about the long term. It had prompted him to take his jeep down to Milwaukee, a city he'd used to enjoy visiting on his way to and from the hut.

His first trip had been in search of solar panels and the accompanying batteries, inverters and cabling. It was something he'd looked into previously, but never gotten round to implementing, so he knew the location of the warehouse that had housed what he was after. It was untouched. People were after food, not arcane electricity generation equipment. He'd been worried about wasting gas, making the drive to Milwaukee, but he'd found an abandoned farm on the outskirts of the city with its own tank. He'd take the occasional trip down to refuel his empty jerry cans, and to reconnoitre the city streets in search of unlooted items that might be of use.

'Hey!' came a yell, and he swung his head round in astonishment, automatically placing his hand on the pistol inside his coat. A young fellow was standing on a third storey balcony, above a barbershop just four shops away from the bakery. 'Twelve days without contact!'

It was apparently a normal greeting for men these days, the number of days you'd been without contact with another human being. Everyone knew the math - four days from infection and you were dead. If you believed them when they said they'd been more than four days without contact, they were safe. Of course, the greeting meant nothing if the speaker was female. No matter how long it had been since their last human interaction, if they were infected they could kill you.

'Too long to count for me,' he called back.

They nodded at each other. The young fellow was clothed in stained denim jeans and a ripped black t-shirt. He looked haggard, a scavenger, just like the maybe-labrador.

The man called out again. 'You the only one in that building?'

'Yup,' came the response. 'We had a dude lose his shit early on the piece. Went postal with an AK47, just rampaging floor to floor, so the whole place emptied out pretty fast.'

'You took him out and claimed the building?'

'Nah, I holed up in my room with the doors triple-locked, and at some point he ran out of ammo and stuck a knife through his eye. Guess I inherited the building by default. You been living in the area?'

'Nope. Been up north; heading back there soon. Where'd everyone go? There were a few more folk wandering last time I was here.'

'Army came through two weeks ago. Said they'd set up a camp somewhere in Illinois for anyone who wanted to come. They were all suited up, testing everyone before they'd allow them to join the convoy. Took a shit-tonne of folk with them.'

'You didn't join 'em?'

'Nope. Just takes one faulty test and that virus'll rip right through whatever camp they've got there. A big group seemed a bad idea. Say, you just travelling by yourself? Want a hand with whatever operation you've got going on?'

'Sorry, son, ain't gonna happen.'

The kid nodded, resigned. 'Good luck then.'

The man backed away down the street, not entirely convinced that a petulant shot in the back wouldn't come. As he reversed his footsteps, he considered what the kid had said. Government camps. Point of entry testing. He had to agree with the kid. Until they found a vaccine, all it would take was one faulty test result…

He rounded the corner, back to where his jeep was waiting. It wasn't long before he was back on the road north. He was noticing the decay in the road with each journey.

Day Nine

Fear had taken over, consuming the nation. Blanket travel bans were now in force. As the virus had moved inland and between the coastal cities that had initially been infected, the federal government had now ordered a complete shutdown of all ports, airports and major roads. Soldiers in bright orange or yellow biohazard suits manned makeshift barricades on motorways out. It wasn't *all* motorways in *all* cities, of course. With the chaos that was unfolding, mobilising a nationwide response was difficult at best. And there were only so many biohazard suits to go round.

It wasn't simply a US problem. The global village being what it was, cases of infection began to soon pop up wherever flights from America landed. There was panic on the streets of London, Sydney, Paris, Kuala Lumpar. SARS and swine flu began to pale into insignificance. It wasn't a strain of the flu, although it did share some of the flu's characteristics. It was an unknown, and it was difficult to fight an unknown.

***

'I have a theory,' Doctor Jewell told her committee. 'Feel free to interrupt whenever you disagree.'

There were nods and mutterings of agreement. The medical members of the committee were for the most part floundering in a sea of data that simply made no sense. It took time to dissect the hows and whys of a new organism. Time was the one thing the virus was not providing.

She grabbed a whiteboard pen, and began to write notes as she spoke. 'First assumption: the virus is manmade. Our DNA work is in its early, early days, but the data I'm seeing strongly suggests that what we're looking at has been spliced together from a number of existing organisms. This virus didn't come out of nowhere through some quirk of nature.

'Second assumption: Parts of what make up this virus don't exist in any lab outside of the military. We're seeing rates of infection and mortality far in excess of anything we've encountered in nature. Ebola? Doesn't even come close. I know we're signatories to the Biological Weapons Convention, but do we really believe that we don't hold supplies of some scary and fundamentally illegal shit?

'Third assumption: Someone inside the military, who really doesn't like society, has gone rogue. With its spread and mortality rate, this is a fucking doomsday virus.' She turned to the bureaucrat. 'I'm hoping you'd have told us if someone had tried to blackmail the government with the release of a virus of this nature.'

The bureaucrat nodded. 'Look, I haven't heard anything like that. From my briefings, the chain of command is as much in the dark as we are.'

'So no extortion attempt, and no one stepping forth to charge for a vaccine that they "just happen to have at their disposal." Okay, bear with me. We have a virus, and we have a Patient Zero. If you accept my three assumptions, our Patient Zero did not acquire the virus through natural means. He's been infected with a purpose.

'So who infected him? The logical candidate is the girl from Ronny's Basement, Joanne Aldercroft. My hypothesis? The virus requires a Y chromosome to activate. Aldercroft is injected with the virus, and at that stage it's inert. She's a woman. She ain't got no Y chromosome. She can walk around for as long as she wants, and nothing's going to happen. Until she sleeps with someone.

'That's part two of the hypothesis. The initial transmission is by sexual activity. So she sleeps with Chris Bretzner, our Patient Zero. And he's certainly got a Y chromosome.'

The bureaucrat was staring at her intently. 'You're saying you think Aldercroft was knowingly injected with the virus?'

'Sure, she might have been infected with the inert virus without her knowledge, and whoever infected her was just waiting for her to sleep with someone, then monitor the results. But you told us she she'd shot a state official in the face on the way out of Boston. I'd say we're entitled to draw a few negative conclusions from that. I think she knew exactly what she was doing. She was a fucking plague ship.

'So. Aldercroft gets the hell out of dodge. She flies to Boston, and whoever's behind all of this, they wait to see what happens. Does it work as expected? Yup. Bretzner goes down in a screaming heap, and begins taking people with him. So far, so good. But will it kill? They're waiting to see what happens to Bretzner, and they get the result they want. Within days he's dead.

'And here's the part that really convinces me that Aldercroft was no innocent player. Within four days of Bretzner's death, we've suddenly got deaths from coast to coast, city after city. Everything was in place, ready to go. They just needed a real life test run. There'll be a Patient Zero in each of those initial cities, and I'll bet they all contracted it sexually on the same night. If Aldercroft was the initial plague ship, they had a whole fleet of them ready to go.'

A usually quiet member of the committee spoke up. 'That would tie in with the mortality stats - men only.'

'Exactly. It needs a Y chromosome to activate, and although it spreads from there to anyone, male or female, it needs a Y chromosome to trigger its attack mode.'

The committee sat in silent. Now that it had been said, it made a hell of a lot of sense.

The bureaucrat leaned back in his seat, fixing his eyes on the ceiling. 'Terrorist attack then?'

'We should assume so.'

Day Twenty-two

Who and why?

They were the big questions.

Doctor Jewell's remarks had been passed up various chains. They explained a lot. What they didn't explain though was motivation and opportunity. It was one thing to buy some fertiliser and wires, and build a car bomb. It was an entirely different proposition to gain access to internationally outlawed biological weapons. And why were they unleashed?

The who and the why had been a mystery. If the virus, either wholly or in part, had come from the US military, Doctor Jewell and her team were never told. Of course, if international treaties had been breached, the government would have been reluctant to admit it. And the virus might well have been sourced from outside of the US. No one would ever know.

The why ended up being answered, at least in part, exactly three weeks after Patient Zero had first walked in to his local medical clinic. A short video was sent to all national and international news outlets, and published on the internet. It featured a woman in silhouette, speaking just two sentences through a vocoder. In case of confusion, the two sentences were subtitled in capitals.

'THE PATRIARCHY HAS BEEN SMASHED. YOU HAD IT COMING.'

THE MARIONETTE

Candice Thornberry was the only daughter of an almost-nouveau riche family. That meant that Candice's grandfather, Arthur Thornberry Senior, had come from nowhere and made a lot of money, and that her father, Arthur Thornberry Junior, liked to pretend that the money had been around for at least a few generations longer.

The source of the money was more than a little mysterious. There was no obvious business that Mr Thornberry the Senior had ever successfully run, but the money had evidently rolled in from somewhere. He had spent his years living quite the high life, and on his death left his son a rather grand house on a rather grand street, a collection of holiday homes in randomly scattered resort towns, a comprehensive investment package of stocks, bonds and equities, and a number of significantly sized bank accounts.

Thornberry the Senior's personal life was as mysterious as his ability to rake in the funds. He had definitely married, for the local registry office confirmed that a young lady named Doris Yealand had said 'I do' on a Saturday morning; one of seven different sets of vows exchanged in that particular registry office that morning. Mr Thornberry the Junior, who had never known his mother, had done some research into her identity, but had gotten nowhere. Of the various Yealands in the area, not a single one had been named Doris, and of the various Doris Yealands he had tracked down from other more far flung areas, none seemed even remotely likely to have been his mother.

Mr Thornberry Junior was still a single man of just twenty-two when his father departed the world, leaving him all alone with just a moderately large fortune to keep him company. Having failed at finding out anything much about either his father or mother, he therefore shrugged, gave up, and found a pretty girl to woo.

The wooing went easily. Being the holder of a large fortune went a long way to assuaging his general lack of good looks and personality. A wedding was soon held and young Candice followed swiftly thereafter (swiftly, of course, being nine months and one week, for anything much swifter may have invited unfavourable comment).

It was just after Candice had been born that her mother began unpacking a number of old wooden crates that had sat for years in what was to become Candice's playroom. The room had once been Thornberry Senior's junk room, and although Thornberry Senior had cleared much of it out following the birth of his son, the collection of wooden crates had simply sat there, stacked against one of the walls, for the whole of Thornberry Junior's childhood and teenage years.

Candice's mother had no intention of allowing this state of affairs to continue through her daughter's formative years. During the glorious moments when her daughter was asleep, she pried the crates open one by one, arranging the contents into piles, ready for her husband to examine at the end of the day.

The contents were curious, to say the least. It was essentially a multitude of strange collectables – old antique pottery, labelled fossils from around the world, shrunken tattooed heads, ancient coins and silverware, and disparate pieces of old-fashioned weaponry, to name but a small selection. It was as if a young man with too much money had simply walked into an antiques store, bought the entire stock with the intention of starting a museum, and then given up the whole exercise as a bad idea. Candice's mother had a sneaking suspicion that was fairly close to the truth.

As it happened, Mr Thornberry Junior decided that a private museum was a fantastic idea. He converted one of the lower rooms of the house into a grotesquely opulent Victorian-style exhibition room, and one by one, the contents of the crates made their way downstairs to feature in his showcase.

There was one item though that never reached the exhibition room: a large marionette, which had once but no longer had strings attached to its arms and legs. It was dressed as a male, with flowing diamond-patterned trousers and a simple white shirt, but its slightly overlong brown hair and slightly effeminate features (sultry eyelashes that had been individually stuck on, and slightly pouting red lips) meant that it could easily have been originally clothed in a flowing dress. It was the sort of toy that a tourist might have brought back from Italy as something a little different from the usual Venetian masquerade masks.

The marionette had been packed in a crate of its own, one that sat at the very bottom of one of the stacks. There was a layer of rumpled fabric beneath the toy, as if to protect it from the rough wooden floor of the crate, but then whoever had nailed the crate shut had presumably failed to check whether anything else had been packed in around it.

Given that Candice's mother was sitting in a playroom, and the marionette was obviously a child's toy, the decision was immediately made to keep the toy in the room. The strings could surely be replaced, and Candice would undoubtedly enjoy hours of entertainment with it once she had the necessary coordination to make it work.

As it happened, the strings never did get replaced. Candice's mother died suddenly of a hitherto undiagnosed heart condition when Candice was one year and three months old, and the succession of nannies who were employed to raise Candice simply placed the marionette on a window sill, where it remained, out of sight and out of mind, for a number of years to come.

Candice could never quite remember just when the marionette first appeared in her dreams. It was certainly after she turned five, but she later she couldn't be sure whether it was six or seven or eight. Regardless of what age she was, the dreams always followed the same format. The marionette would rise from its position on the windowsill and, despite its lack of strings, leap to the ground and walk jerkily across the carpeted floor. It would make its way out of the playroom (Candice, on waking, could never quite recall whether the playroom door was always open or whether the marionette somehow managed to work the doorknob), enter her bedroom and sit beside her on the edge of her pillow.

And every night that it made its way to her room, it would tell her things, secrets of future events and people that she did not yet know. When she would wake, she could not recall any of the things the marionette had told her. Just as with all of her dreams, the details had faded by sunrise, lost to the night that had been.

The curious thing was that although at the time the dreams often seemed frightening, in the morning she could never quite remember why. Perhaps it was simply the lack of remembered detail; after all, the way that the marionette moved in her dreams was quite comical – presumably, the fear came from what it had whispered to her.

Everything changed one day when Candice was about twelve. The occasion was when a new girl joined Candice's class at school. As the girl was introduced to the class, Candice knew with an absolute certainty that the new girl was a thief, a thief with a passion for stealing food and money from other students' schoolbags. *How* she knew this, she could not have said. And then, with a strange clarity, she recalled being told all about it by the marionette. She could remember the precise detail of every one of the marionette's words that night; and the face that she was now staring at, there at the front of the class, was the same face that somehow, years ago, the marionette had implanted in her brain and that her brain had then hidden.

When she arrived home, she ran straight upstairs, into the room where the marionette sat. Candice couldn't recall the last time anyone had actually moved the marionette. It had sat on its shelf for as long as she could remember, untouched and undusted, and yet, there was not a speck of dust on it. She retreated from the room. It wasn't that she was scared. The doll didn't move in the daytime. It couldn't hurt anyone. Nonetheless, she didn't want to pick the doll up, and she didn't want to be in the same room as it.

Two weeks later, the new girl was suspended, caught stealing from the schoolbags of her fellow classmates. For the first time, Candice truly began to feel afraid. 'Knowledge' from a dream had been quantified, a sinister deja vu.

A month later, she looked over at another girl in her class – a girl called Melissa, whom Candice had known since they were both nine – and abruptly knew, beyond a shadow of a doubt, that the girl was sleeping with an eighteen year old. She knew the name of the eighteen year old – PJ Baker, a kid who worked at a vineyard, having dropped out of school the previous year. Candice was spared the details of the romance, which was presumably a relief for one who was just twelve. Nonetheless, she knew enough – that the relationship had been going on for three months, for instance. Why she knew this *now*, she could not say. She'd known Melissa for three years, and yet suddenly now was the time she learned that Melissa had been screwing PJ Baker for three months? It was as if a room had existed in her brain for years, but the door to the room had only just been unlocked and opened. She knew what had created the room – she could suddenly recall the marionette whispering it all to her as she lay in her bed – but why the door had suddenly been opened was beyond her.

That night, she shut the door on the room that contained the marionette. It didn't stop her dreaming the same thing that she dreamt almost every night, as the marionette still somehow managed to reach her room. She shouldn't have assumed that a closed door would be an obstacle, given that a lack of strings clearly wasn't an impediment to the doll moving.

As the weeks and months passed, the visits continued. As usual, Candice could recall nothing about the detail. It was enough to know that she had been visited. Information had been imparted, though the moment when she would remember receiving the information was anyone's guess. The revelations also continued, as did the confirmations that the revelations were accurate. Six weeks later, Melissa's parents complained to the police, and PJ Baker was charged with statutory rape.

And Candice discovered more and more things that she didn't want to know. Dishonesty. Sex crimes. Terrible acts of violence. It wasn't just her fellow schoolmates. It was family friends that her father invited round for drinks or dinner – a business associate of her father's who had a cocaine addiction and had smashed the kneecaps of a trade competitor. It was relatives – an uncle who had slept with a female neighbour, and, on a separate occasion, the female neighbour's husband. It was one of the local police officers who had turned up to talk to the class, who had been stealing drugs from the evidence locker.

She began keeping a record of the offences that were revealed and the punishments, if any, that would unfold. As time wore on, Candice became more and more accustomed to the information that she would receive. For the most part, justice would ensue. Police would become involved, or significant others would take whatever steps were necessary. Yet there was still a sizeable minority of remembered events for which there were no repercussions for the offender.

Candice became aware of sins and crimes that a girl her age had no business knowing about. Sometimes they caused nightmares in their own right, never mind the half-remembered visitations of the marionette that occurred every other night. Occasionally though, the information that she received would prove useful. Knowing the never-convicted-but-nonetheless-criminal history of her P.E. teacher meant that turning down private after-school tuition was an easy decision. A year later, knowing that her two-years-older suitor was a rapist was a more than adequate reason to spurn his advances. Two years later, she felt no compunction in saying no to an offer to babysit her father's friend's children. She'd briefly met the man at one of her father's parties, and already knew what he had done to one of his previous babysitters prior to dropping her home.

When Candice was seventeen, her entire life disintegrated. As she almost immediately admitted to police, she walked into her father's study, raised the pistol that she had removed from his desk drawer the previous evening, and shot him in the head. One shot was all it took. She gave no reason as to why she had pulled the trigger on her father. Despite the proddings of her lawyers (one of whom would have blushed mightily if he had been aware of her sudden knowledge of what he had done with his sister the previous year), she refused to defend the charge of murder in any way, shape or form, and was sentenced accordingly.

It was a media field day – the tall (for her age), impassive seventeen year old being led into court; the speculation as to why the crime had been committed. It didn't hurt that the family was wealthy. Everyone loved a good whydunnit involving protagonists with money. It also didn't hurt that Candice was attractive. The public definitely loved the spectacle of a pretty girl accused of murder.

Candice appeared in court on a total of just three occasions. Firstly, on her arrest, she was granted bail to the home of an uncle. The conservative elements of the media were outrage. How dare an (alleged) murderess be bailed? The liberal media were of the opposite persuasion. An attractive seventeen year old? Innocent until proven guilty? Who knew what sins the father had committed against his angelic daughter!

Secondly, there was the entry of the guilty plea. At this point, Candice was remanded back into custody. A guilty plea to murder meant a jail sentence was inevitable. The frenzied speculation continued. Was the girl insane? A psychiatric report was directed. No, said the report writer, Candice was not insane. She seemed entirely rational, extremely intelligent, and utterly lucid. She did not however wish to discuss her motivations for executing her father. That was for her, and her alone, to know.

Thirdly and finally, there was the date of sentencing. The cameras were everywhere, reporters breathlessly reporting on such highly pertinent details such as what the defendant was wearing when she appeared in the dock (a simple, modest, knee-length black dress, for what it was worth). The judge – a most experienced and pragmatic individual – was evidently well-acquainted with the rumours that the deceased father had been engaging in unsavoury intimacies with his daughter, and had paid the price. The resulting mandatory minimum sentence was the lowest the country had ever seen for murder. The crown had no interest in appealing. They had merely gone through the motions, entirely certain that a bad man had received his just desserts.

When Candice Thornberry was released from prison, it was after her first parole hearing. She had been a model prisoner, and her risk of reoffending was deemed to be low. By then, the media had long since moved on to other many and varied *causes celebres*. Little to no fanfare accompanied her release. She kept her head down and changed her name.

She never went back to the site of her old family home, not that she would have recognised it anymore. It had long since been sold and turned into a housing development. The contents of the house – all of her father's treasures – had been bundled up and sold at auction. The house had been bowled, swept away by a tide of heavy machinery.

Candice never spoke to anyone of her gift or curse. And she certainly never spoke of her sudden knowledge, all those years ago, that her father was a member of a ring of international paedophiles, a monster who preyed on young boys. She had walked to his desk, removed and loaded the pistol that she knew he kept there, and had destroyed the destroyer of so many lives.

And she tried never to think about the marionette, sitting now on another child's shelf, walking on stringless legs each night, and filling another head with endless visions of other people's sins.

OUT OF PHASE

Years ago, back when I was in late High School, I used to compete in a Speech and Drama competition. To the average observer, it was as bad as you might think. Children and teens, of wildly differing talent, performing poems, prose, monologues et al of wildly differing standards. Many were terrible. It was barely worth sitting through the dross to witness the items of beauty.

Nonetheless, I loved the dross. I was competitive. A field of dross vastly heightened my chances of prize money.

There *was* a secondary joy to the yearly event though. The competitors didn't just come from the small city where I lived. They also came from the other smaller towns that surrounded us, and once a year I would get to meet one particular girl that I had lusted after for years. Her name was Alice. She was my height (tall for a girl) and thin, with long, brown-blonde hair. She had the most expressive face I had ever encountered, and she walked like she controlled everything around her. She was the same age as me, which meant that our paths should have crossed every so often in other forums - debating competitions or inter-school sports days (I was always rather more proficient at the debating than the sports) - but they never did. It was always only on that once a year Speech and Drama competition.

The competition itself lasted two and a half days - Friday from after school until some time on Sunday evening. For most of the year, I would happily fantasise about the girls at my own school (and God knows that certainly kept me occupied), but for those three days my imagination belonged solely to Alice. In terms of the running of the competition, the younger children would dominate the mornings and afternoons, while the older age brackets would fill the evenings. Both Alice and I were saddled with younger siblings, so we both tended to end up whiling away the hours during the day. Sometimes that meant I could get her on her own. Most times, there was an ever-shifting group of us backstage or in the corridors.

The venue was always the city's Council-owned theatre. It was a sprawling building, based around the main stage and its three levels of audience seating. In and around the theatre proper were the seemingly endless rooms that made up the rest of the building: the box office, the practice rooms, a conference section, the management offices. But best of all was the network of backstage corridors. They seemed to enclose the whole theatre in a labyrinth of hidden tunnels. A corridor might suddenly dart up a flight of stairs, ending in a lighting box high above the audience. Another corridor might duck beneath the stage itself, allowing those of us who had followed it to giggle about the possibility of banging on the boards above our heads and crawling off, leaving a fellow competitor flailing distractedly for his or her lines.

I vividly remember the final year that I competed in the competition. I had managed to get Alice alone. It was the final night, the Sunday night, and we had both finished our Shakespearean characterisations. I was still dressed as Bottom from *A Midsummer Night's Dream*, while Alice was Ophelia. She wore a flowing, ankle-length, white dress. Although it sported a high neck, much of the upper bodice was sufficiently lacy to capture my attention every time she leaned forward.

There were at least a half dozen entrants still to come in that class - Shakespeare was popular that year - and it was to be immediately followed by an equally large class from the age group below us, though they were reading from Dickens rather than performing Shakespearean dress-up. There was time to kill. Somehow, despite the fact that I was wearing pantaloons and a silk shirt with lace sleeves, I persuaded Alice that we should explore one of the backstage tunnels. It was one of the lighting tunnels, that accelerated upwards in a series of staircases and allowed access to all sorts of high places. Technically, it should probably have been locked off, access verboten to us unruly teenagers. And to a certain extent it was. Yet there was always an unlocked door somewhere, that would offer access to a corridor that would loop back to another corridor, and another door, and another door, and *that* door would be unlocked.

So Alice and I gained access to the lighting tunnel. We made our way up a series of staircases, her holding the bottom of her dress so that she didn't trip, me imagining what lay beneath her dress. After a few corridors and corners and further sets of stairs, we found ourselves in a small plywood crawlspace. We made our way to the end, peering through the lighting rig to the small audience - looking even smaller from our vantage point - and the solitary figure on stage. At that height, we could barely hear what was happening. It looked like a kid playing Julius Caesar, but I couldn't be certain.

We shuffled back. Even in this unlit wooden box, high above the theatre world, Alice and I could still see each other relatively easily. I tried to make small talk, complimenting her on her braids. I'd always been rubbish at small talk. Then suddenly, she was leaning in and kissing me, and I tried to keep up, tried to work out what in the hell my tongue should or should not be doing.

The world went black. Every light in the theatre went out at once, and I heard the mock screams from those below. Cut the lights on any crowd and they'll scream. The power cut lasted just a few seconds, before normality was restored. In those few seconds, I had pulled back from Alice - a foolish thing to have done, as sudden darkness was surely there to be embraced. When the light returned she was gone.

I remember staring about me in utter confusion. One second she was there, the next she was gone. It was a narrow area, impossible for her to have slipped past me in such a short time. And yet, there I was - alone.

A terrible thought abruptly occurred to me, and I crab-walked to the edge of the box, half-expecting to see a body splayed out on the red-cushioned seats below. The seats were empty. Alice had simply disappeared.

I slowly made my way back down through the series of staircases and corridors up which Alice and I had initially travelled. I had half-convinced myself that she must have somehow made it past me; that the blackout must have been for longer than I had thought; that I would come across her on my way back down. I didn't. Our next competition class - impromptu speeches - came and went. She didn't show. I was preoccupied by her non-appearance, and embarrassed myself with a particularly shambling performance. Awards were distributed. There was still no sign of Alice. By this point, her parents had left the audience and begun a backstage search. It proved fruitless.

I said nothing. Frankly, I was panicked, having seemingly been the last person to see her. I'd been making out with her, away from all and sundry. And now she was missing. I may have been young and naive, but I could see how that might have looked.

The police investigation into Alice's disappearance drew a blank. She had played Ophelia, drifted backstage, and vanished. We were all quizzed, us amateur teenage thespians, and I was of no use. I told police that I dimly remembered being in one of the dressing rooms, and, as it turned out, one of my fellow competitors also dimly remembered me being there with him. Never trust the human brain to provide an accurate recollection of events.

There investigation ended up focussing on whether Alice might have left the building and been abducted. Certainly, most of us performers had at one time or another walked through the backstage exit door and found ourselves accidentally locked out of the theatre. Police concluded that this was the only likely possibility. Accidental lockout. Strange man in car park. Goodbye Alice. There were no cameras in the area to prove or disprove the hypothesis.

The only person who knew that the police conclusion was utterly wrong was me. I'd been there, lips locked, moments before she vanished. As much as I may have tried to convince myself that she must surely have slipped past me into the endless backstage corridors, in my heart of hearts I knew it could not have occurred. Something had happened that was far beyond my understanding.

I quit Speech and Drama lessons. If I had continued, I would surely have been forced to return for the following year's competition. The last thing I wanted was to set foot again in that building. The competition continued, regardless. Security guards were hired to patrol the car parks and exits. No one was abducted.

Nonetheless, the competition made headlines, and not for the quality of its performances. On the Sunday night, Alice apparently appeared briefly on stage. A girl was massacring the role of Lady Macbeth when Alice flickered into existence. She was still wearing her Ophelia costume, her hair braided. The audience gasped, screamed, but Alice didn't seem to see or hear them. Instead, staring wildly about her, she screamed, 'Where the fuck are you all?' Then she disappeared.

I wasn't there. I didn't see her. I talked to some of those who *were* there though, and they told me that she sounded utterly terrified. They told me it was definitely Alice. They'd seen her year by year, growing up, knew exactly what she'd looked like. That she had appeared on stage, a year after after her vanishing act, was of course impossible, and the newspapers published stories hinting at mass dramatic hysteria.

It didn't end there. Every so often, Alice would be seen to appear, sometimes on stage, sometimes in other parts of the building; seen sometimes by a crowd, sometimes by almost no one. The only unifying aspects of what was described were her costume - her long flowing dress - and that she was in terror, alone. The theatre became a byword for bad luck. Quality productions from out of town stayed away. The conference facilities decreased in popularity. No one wanted a screaming ghost-girl appearing in the middle of proceedings.

Two years after Alice disappeared, I finished High School, left town and moved on to university. I'm two years into a Commerce degree, the sort of degree you do when you have no idea where you want to end up, but you don't want to sink as low as an Arts degree. In between my studies, I've spent a lot of time trying to understand what could possibly have happened to Alice. My bookshelf has a lot of volumes devoted to both the supernatural and to theoretical physics. The sideline studies haven't helped. I still have no idea what could possibly have occurred. My best explanation is that she somehow ended up out of phase with the rest of the world. Don't ask me what that means though. It still fails to make any sense to me either. At the end of the day, it's just a series of words that I took from a book about the Philadelphia Experiment, where the US Navy allegedly made a Destroyer invisible back in 1943. I don't pretend to offer a correlation between a US Navy experiment that probably never occurred and a teenage girl disappearing from the inside of a theatre.

I read somewhere the other day that the theatre is due to be demolished. It's not making money any more. I wonder what will happen in whatever reality Alice inhabits when the bulldozers move in. I hope she'll receive closure, in whatever form that may be.

THE PARABLE OF THE YOUNG MAN WITHOUT SIN

There was once a man who was about to be stoned to death. His crimes were many and varied, but had not previously been committed in the community in which he was about to die, for the man was a traveller. He had many enemies, and had moved on from many places (often in a great hurry), but on this occasion he had not moved on fast enough.

As the crowd gathered, rocks in hand, the man cried out, calling on he who was without sin to cast the first stone. He was perhaps not expecting a great reaction, having resigned himself to a slow and painful death, but his words sparked a consternation among the assembled masses. 'Who amongst us is indeed truly without sin?' came a murmur that spread like wildfire. 'Can we throw the stone that will kill a man, when we ourselves are sinful beings?'

And as the crowd conferred, it was decided that within the township there was indeed one without sin. He was a tall, thin young man, with an angelic mop of blonde curls, and as he was brought from his home to stand before the people of the town, a crescendo of excitement grew. For no one could indeed recall a single instance of the young man ever committing a single sin. He was never wrathful, nor was he lazy. One had only to look at his frame to know that gluttony seemed not to trouble him. Nor could anyone recall him envying the position of others; and the thought of him lusting after any of the town's women or men was enough to bring about paroxysms of laughter, for such was his chaste reputation.

Here indeed was one in a position to cast the first stone.

Explaining his duty, the crowd pressed a rock into the puzzled youth's hand. As he was about to undertake his sacred duty and hurl the rock at the soon to be deceased man, the man cried out. 'Let me address him, pray!' was the cry, and the crowd yielded.

'Are you really as free of sin as they say?' asked the man.

'I am, sir,' replied the youth (displaying a suitable level of respect for his elder). 'Sometimes,' and he smiled shyly, 'I almost believe that I might be the Second Coming of the Messiah.'

'Aha!' roared the man. 'Pride! He is afflicted with the sin of pride!'

The crowd gazed at the youth in a new light. And a thought passed through the crowd, as if the crowd were one, that what they really hated was smug young people.

And the first stone was flung, but at the youth, not the young man.

And so so it came to pass that the man was allowed to walk free, while the angelic-haired youth was buried in an unmarked grave at the edge of town, mourned only by his parents.

THE TROUBLE WITH TIME TRAVEL

First test.

The maths worked, according to the computer programme he had constructed from scratch. The testing process had been exhaustive, simulation after simulation after simulation. For a long time, he hadn't dared believe it, instead choosing to run yet another round of testing. Time travel was possible. Now all Xavier Higgins needed to do was prove it.

The time machine had been constructed in Xavier's garden shed. In effect, the shed *was* the time machine. Xavier sat in the centre, surrounded by flickering componentry and vast bundles of exposed wiring. Tapping away at a basic computer keyboard and staring into a small monitor, he set a date. Then, with a deep breath, he hit a large green button, and sank back in his seat.

The world churned around him.

***

The trouble with travelling forward in time is that you cannot predict what will be there when you arrive. In Xavier's case, following his and his shed's mysterious disappearance, the house was sold six months later. The new owner planted a totara tree on the site where the shed once sat. In one hundred and fifty years time, the totara was around twenty-five metres high and several metres wide. It was an impressive specimen.

When Xavier's shed attempted to coalesce in the exact spot occupied by the one hundred and fifty year old totara, the results were catastrophic. The shed seemed to simultaneously explode and implode as the trunk of the tree became the centre of a continuity cataclysm.

In the weeks that followed, the surrounding populace tried to make sense of what had occurred. There was wreckage everywhere, inexplicable items scattered across the neighbouring properties: wooden boards, circuitry, splintered pieces of sheet metal.

The totara had spent days as a smoking, splintered wreck. It had toppled in the impossible explosion, and those tasked with its removal struggled to comprehend how human remains could possibly be embedded in the tree's heartwood.

NEW ZEALAND GOTHIC

I was at a party in a garage, when Bryce showed up, looking shaken. We were in Inner Kaiti, one of Gisborne's central-ish suburbs, not that Gisborne was large enough to have too many *outer* suburbs. It was a garage party for two reasons. Firstly, Kaiti was devoid of pubs - you had to head into the CBD for those. Secondly, my mate Gary had a two car garage, but no car. He'd been caught drink driving twice within five years and had had the government confiscate his old Honda Accord, so he'd laid down some carpet over the garage concrete, bought a beer fridge and set up a few tables. It had become a favourite neighbourhood hangout. As a bonus, Gary never had to drive home.

When Bryce made his appearance, he was about a half hour late, which was most uncharacteristic. He was a man who could usually be relied upon to arrive early, already drinking from his second or third bottle of beer. Here he was though, late and without beer. He looked a mess, wide-eyed and dishevelled, sweating as if he had run all the way here.

There were about four or five of us already present, and we raised howls of derision.

He smiled weakly. 'Sorry, guys. Running a bit late. You know how it goes.'

'What about the beer? You being a cheapskate on us?'

'Aw, come on, crack me one open, someone. I'll bring two boxes next time.'

Someone relented, and Bryce stood there with a beer in hand. General conversation restarted. I sidled over. 'You okay, mate? You look bloody terrible.'

He brushed away my concern, hinting at an unexpectedly busy schedule, but providing no details. I was becoming intrigued. Bryce was a generally uncomplicated fellow. He worked eight-thirty to five as a council contractor; with the council as his boss, overtime was never on the cards. He had a few exes, but none of the convoluted, tangled variety, and he was lucky enough to have never accidentally ended up with kids. He liked beer, and he liked fishing, and he liked watching rugby league or motor racing. Bryce was as uncomplicated as it got. Which is why I was concerned. Bryce didn't run anywhere. And he certainly didn't show up to garage parties with no beer.

I steered him outside. It was early summer, not quite daylight savings, and the light was already fading fast. It was a beautiful evening, still and clear. A couple of the local kids were steadfastly continuing to ride their bikes in circles on the road outside, ignoring parental calls to come inside for dinner.

We stood there silently, contemplating the geometric patterns of the cyclists, and taking in the murmur of voices (and occasional outbursts of laughter or profanity) from the garage. Bryce seemed lost in his thoughts. 'Haven't seen you run in a long time, mate,' I said, breaking the conversational ice.

'Eh? Oh. Yeah, hope I don't have to again for a while, bro!'

He grinned, but it was only half-hearted.

'Everything okay?'

A pause.

'Yeah, bro.'

'It's just, you looked a bit freaked, mate, you know, like you'd seen some shit you didn't wanna see.'

'Nah, bro, I'm all good.'

It took a while, but I finally broke him down.

'Okay,' he finally said, 'there's a story, yeah, but you ain't gonna believe it.'

'Try me.'

'So I've just left home. I've got my beers, I've walked out the end of Darwin Road, and I'm heading down De Lautour. I'm just about to turn down Owen Road, and I see this group of people standing there, four of them. They reminded me of that painting, American Gothic, standing looking at me with these long, gaunt faces. They were all wearing cloaks, which was just weird. It was like four old geezers had mis-timed Halloween. I was walking towards them, trying not to stare, when one of them suddenly says, "We should not be here."

'I stopped walking, thinking they were talking to me. Still not sure whether they were or not. But they just kind of stood there, staring at me. I was trying to work out what was going on. Were they, like, escaped dementia patients or something? I was trying to think how far away the nearest rest home was. I couldn't place the accent of the one who'd spoken - figured they were some kind of Eastern Europeans - and they looked thin as hell, not that I could see much of them other than their faces, what with their cloaks.

'So I was thinking they might be starving or something, they seemed that thin. And I was feeling generous, so I asked whether I could get them some fish and chips.'

'You were going to let them make you late for beers?'

'Well, I was thinking I'd just order the meal and leave them to it, but they didn't seem to understand what I was doing. So I walked down to the chip shop and ordered a couple of scoops, and just sort of waited until it was done. I'd pop out every so often, just to make sure they were still there, and they were. Anyway, the chips got cooked, and I took them back to the group, and that's when shit got fucked up.

'I handed one of them the chips - they all looked pretty much the same, so it was hard to say whether he was the one who'd spoken earlier - but he just dropped them, like he didn't know what to do with them. Then, just as I was about to step back in and pick them up, all four of them dropped to their knees and bent in towards the chips. It was bloody terrifying. Their mouths just seemed to unhinge, and this crazy as all hell second mouth emerged. They had two sets of circular teeth-things, that were grinding in opposite directions, just hoovering up the chips and grinding them up as they passed through.'

I had been listening to Bryce's story, wondering where he was going with it, but that was a twist I hadn't seen coming. I stared at him dubiously through narrowed eyes. Was he taking the piss, or was he high? He didn't *look* high though, and frankly he'd never been one for anything much other than beer.

'Yeah, I know it sounds like a tall story,' he said, 'but I know what I saw. It scared the bejeezus out of me. I just dropped my box of beer and freakin' ran. Made it here, and had to put up with everyone's shit for being late with no beer.'

'Hell of an excuse for turning up with no piss…'

Bryce stood there, beer in hand, staring out at the rapidly disappearing light. His face was pinched, his forehead creased with worry lines. 'I just watched a mouth come out of another mouth,' he finally said, spitting out the words in a fit of fear and disgust.

'How does that even work?' I asked, fascinated despite myself; disbelieving, but wanting to hear the tale in its fullness.

'It was like a thick tube of muscle,' said Bryce, after some thought. 'And then the two sets of rotating teeth at the end. Imagine an open mouth, but perfectly round. And then another round set of teeth, taking up all the open space inside the mouth, with the two sets of teeth spinning in opposite directions, so that everything that was sucked through had to be ground to a pulp between them. They were pretty damned efficient, too. Those chips were disappearing at a rate of knots. I wonder what they'd do to a hunk of meat?'

Bryce finished his beer. He gazed at the empty bottle, while I stared intently at the ground.

'Shit,' he said. 'I shouldn't have told you this. You think I'm nuts.'

'It's a lot to take in…'

'Just don't repeat the story, okay? Don't want everyone thinking I'm a loose unit.'

And with that, Bryce disappeared back inside. He avoided me for the rest of the evening, and left early, taking a taxi. That was another un-Bryce-like action - he *always* walked home.

When I made my own exit, maybe an hour after Bryce had departed, I followed my usual route, until I ended up on the corner of Owen Road and De Lautour Road. The fish and chip shop was on the opposite side of the road to me, perhaps twenty metres away to my left. Ordinarily, I'd have turned in the direction of the fish and chip shop, making my way townwards, but something made me turn to the right and cross the road. I walked perhaps twenty or thirty metres back up De Latour Road towards Darwin Road, retracing Bryce's steps.

There, in the middle of the footpath, was the brightly-coloured cardboard box that would have earlier in the evening contained Bryce's beer. There were several smashed bottles, pieces stilled mingling damply with the cardboard. The bottles that had survived the fall had evidently been uplifted by opportunists who had arrived on the scene later. Against a nearby wire fence that was overgrown with ivy were a few sheets of newspaper, blown there in the mild evening breeze. I examined them by the light of my phone. They were covered with the greasy film of fatty food.

I heard the sound of movement, rustling noises in a nearby garden. It could have been nothing more than a possum or hedgehog, but I was suddenly in no mood to be taking chances. I ran, hightailing it in the direction of home.

It's been a few weeks now since that party in Gary's garage. There's been another one since, and I caught a taxi there and back. I noticed Bryce did too.

Kaiti has always had a problem with feral dogs. They roam everywhere, not generally dangerous, but a huge annoyance, especially to traffic. The local council's dog control officers seemed to have largely given up on trying to deal with them. You had to have basically caught one before the dog control squad would come around and put in an appearance. I haven't seen many stray dogs though lately, not since Gary's party.

Bryce's words keep ringing in my ears: *I wonder what they'd do to a hunk of meat?*

POSSESSION

It was a quiet night at the Fourth Street Gentlemen's Jazz Club. The live band, a fiery acid-jazz outfit who had thrown together a more alternative set for the midweek crowd, had wound up for the night. The low, heavenly sound of John Coltrane bid the clientele goodnight as they departed in dribs and drabs into the city streets.

It was the time of night when men get reflective, maybe even somber, and the four old men at their regular table were doing just that.

'Did you hear about Julian?' one of them asked.

There was a general depressed nodding of heads.

'Who'd have thought it, eh?'

'And he was coming on so well with his saxophone. That solo he blew at open mic night last month - astounding...'

'There're still some questions about exactly what happened,' said the originator of the discussion, who was obviously fishing for rumours. 'A decidedly odd business, it seems.'

'I blame it all on that Rupert fellow,' was the judgment of one of the men. 'He was always singing rock, never jazz... I don't like that in a man.'

One of the old men had said nothing and the other three turned to face him. He had the air of a man who was pondering something meaningful. He tapped his fingers on the table, averted his eyes and waited. There was a long silence as the group examined the dregs of their beer, until finally, the silence was broken.

'I heard,' said the man, 'that Rupert was indeed to blame and like you, I too was unsurprised. Never trust a man who listens not to jazz… But the facts of the case were even more disturbing than I could possibly have guessed at. Rupert's villainy knows no bounds! But sit back, my friends, and I shall reveal all…'

***

Julian was not, by nature, a violent man. He was a mild-mannered, charming sort of chap who always fitted in perfectly at civilised dinner parties where sparkling, witty conversation would be required. He listened to jazz (indeed his Miles Davis collection was the envy of all at the Fourth Street Gentlemen's Jazz Club), he gave willingly to charity, and his taste in trilby hats had drawn critical acclaim at the races no less than two weeks ago.

But every Superman has his kryptonite, just as every Caesar has his Brutus. For Julian had found, to his horror, his nemesis – the one man who could drive him over the edge of sanity.

The nemesis, a man by the name of Rupert, was Julian's lodger, and a more annoying individual was impossible to find. He was a short, weedy little fellow with a suspicious resemblance to a dead ferret. That however was not the annoying part. The truly annoying aspect of Rupert's personality was that he was a human jukebox. Due to some hideous genetic defect, Rupert seemed completely unable to listen to a sentence without singing a line from a song that involved at least one word from the sentence.

If you asked him, for instance, to shift his car, you might hear the Beatles' *Baby, Can You Drive My Car*. If you asked whether there was anything to eat in the fridge he might launch into the first line of David Bowie's *Young Americans*. And if you were foolish enough to mention the weather you would likely be subjected to bilge relating to the rain in Spain.

Obviously, this placed a great deal of mental strain upon the unfortunate Julian, but he held up well, until one fateful day…

All he had wanted was to have the fire lit. He did not deserve *Great Balls Of Fire*. With great restraint, Julian stated, 'Rupert, I can't take this anymore. This is the end of the road.'

There is an REM song entitled *It's The End Of The World As We Know It*. Rupert went there.

'As if the singing weren't enough, Rupert, you haven't even paid your rent for the last two weeks!'

The last thing Julian wished to hear at that point was an excerpt from John Lee Hooker's *House Rent Blues*, be it by way of Mr Hooker's original or George Thoroughgood's mash-up that became *One Bourbon, One Scotch, One Beer*. Unfortunately, such an excerpt was exactly what Julian received.

For the uninitiated, both *House Rent Blues* and *One Bourbon, One Scotch, One Beer* are brilliant songs, when sung by either John Lee Hooker or George Thoroughgood. When sung by one such as Rupert however, the experience became somewhat less endearing.

Deep within the neural impulses of Julian's deeply civilised brain, something animal snapped. In a primitive rage, he stalked to the living room wall and grabbed down his father's old Winchester. From a desk drawer came a handful of shells, and with a terrible fury Julian took aim and pulled the trigger. There was a thunderous crash, a haze of smoke and Rupert collapsed with a gaping hole in his chest.

As the smoke cleared and the primal fog lifted from Julian's mind, he suddenly realised what he had done. Choking back a cry of horror, he fell to his knees, trying to avert his eyes from the bloodied corpse that lay before him. For a brief moment he tried to convince himself that Rupert would suddenly sit up and begin the chorus, but the moment quickly passed as the stench of blood assailed his nostrils.

And then, just as the sense of horror had reached its peak, Julian felt an odd change come over him. It was as if something foreign had suddenly smothered his mind and made it its own. He could feel himself there, but he wasn't himself anymore. His eyes looked out at the carnage that he had wrought, but the world seemed misty, not quite real.

He remained on his knees, breathing deeply, and it was a surprise to find himself suddenly standing and covering Rupert's body with a sheet. He could not remember moving, but the movement had clearly happened.

And then his lips began to move of their own accord, despite his frantic attempts to stop them. *Happiness Is A Warm Gun* was never the best song off the Beatles' classic so-called "White Album". Hell, Rupert didn't even particularly *like* the Beatles. Nonetheless, there he was, singing away.

The song faded away and he found himself speaking. 'The vocal chords are a bit rusty there, Julian, but we'll soon have them straightened out…'

His mind screamed in horror, but his mind was buried deep. Instead, he could feel Rupert's spirit and will pressing down upon him, the dead man making Julian's still-living body his own.

Back and forth went the silent battle, both minds struggling for control over the one physical body. And in a sudden crushing moment, Julian realised that Rupert would never stop. Even if the living conquered the dead on this one occasion, Rupert would still be there, lurking, ready to attack again. And would Julian have any defences while he slept? Rupert had resisted the call to whichever plane of existence he had been destined and would not rest until he had revenged himself on Julian in the most complete way possible.

This realisation, and the loathing and horror that came with it, lent Julian a sudden strength that he had never known he had, and for a brief moment he had full and unrestricted control of his body. With his last seconds of freedom he raised the gun to his head and opened his mouth. Somewhere deep inside him he could hear Rupert's silent scream and he felt a bizarre sense of satisfaction in the knowledge that he would be ending the struggle on his own terms.

And with an earth-shattering crash and a split-second flash of light, it was all over. Julian's body swayed backwards and by the time it came to rest, was utterly empty. The two spirits had fled, called to some place else. There had been no winners and there had been no losers. There was merely emptiness and a silent lounge.

***

The old man finished speaking and there was a shocked silence. The facts of the case had indeed been disturbing. But the man who had brought the whole subject up wore a puzzled look on his wrinkled old face. 'Who was there to document this?' he asked.

'Well,' said the storyteller, 'there are admittedly certain facts that are open to conjecture...'

'It's just that I don't see how any of this could be known if the only occupants of the room were Julian and Rupert!'

'Well, the placement of the bodies and other such circumstantial evidence does fit the scenario quite well...'

'But you'll admit that it's also quite possible that Julian merely shot Robert and then, feeling guilty, shot himself?'

'Well of course I do! But that doesn't make nearly so good a story now, does it? Would an ordinary tale of murder and guilty suicide be fitting for a night such as this? Johnny Coltrane deserves more...'

The heckler hung his head in shame. 'Of course, my friend... Well said, you're absolutely right... Poor Julian, what a way to go...'

IN THE WALL

It's been a long time since Kevin disappeared. Decades even. There were just three of us who saw what happened. I haven't seen the other two - Nick and Tate - in at least ten years. After I left Gisborne we fragmented, and our meetings were accidental and awkward, then not at all. I wouldn't even know if they're still alive these days.

I'd moved down to Gisborne from Auckland in the early nineties. I was in my very early twenties, just a few years out of school. My old man had gotten me a job back in the city, working construction, but at that point in life I wasn't crash hot on getting up in the mornings. Figuring I had my whole existence ahead of me to find a career, I'd packed it all in and followed my mate Nick to Gisborne. It was the surf that drew us. We were mad keen surfers, and it didn't get much better than Gizzy. You could almost take your pick of the beaches. Waves to die for, and - away from the two main beaches - you nearly had them to yourself.

I'd picked up enough basic construction skills in Auckland that I could have walked straight into a job in Gisborne, but I hadn't come down to work. Back in those days, it was a piece of piss to hop on the dole, and that's just what I did. If I needed the occasional injection of capital, there were always short-term cash jobs available. What the taxman didn't know never hurt him. It was a great first year. The East Coast was growing more cannabis than it was possible to smoke, the waves were amazing, and we all did just enough casual work to ensure that beer could be bought regularly.

I met Tate through Nick. I think his real name was Joe, but everyone called him Tate because it was short for potato, which was what he looked like. He was Gisborne born and bred. His parents owned a saw-milling company, which was destined to become his, but in a haze of waves and reefers, Tate was doing his best to evade destiny.

Kevin was Tate's right-hand man, though without the destiny issues. No one was leaving Kevin a lucrative inheritance. His dad had been an alcoholic who'd been found floating under one of Gisborne's many bridges, a year after his mum had missed a corner while driving back into town from the (long since burnt down) Tatapouri pub. A few months after his dad's death, Kevin dropped out of school and got a job picking squash, then sweetcorn, then squash again. It was long hours and hard work, and once he was old enough, he hit the dole like the rest of us.

Surf, weed, booze. It was an incredible existence. We were young, and the dole covered our rent and other basic essentials. A day of casual labour here and there covered our beer, and the occasional additional day or two every so often might be required for extras such as a new surfboard.

One day, the four of us had headed up the coast. Tate had a car, an old Holden that had been a gift from his parents. It was unregistered, but traffic cops were few and far between.

That day, we'd hit the road early, as the surf was supposed to be pumping up at Tolaga Bay. It wasn't, so we headed further up the coast on a whim, in search of something better. The forecasts had been wrong, so we bought a box or three of beer in Tokomaru Bay, drank one of them on the beach, and puttered back to Gisborne early afternoon.

We were halfway between Toko' and Tolaga, when Nick suddenly called out to Tate to pull over. As we ground to a halt, waiting for

Nick to announce that he needed to spew, he asked instead, 'What the fuck was that back there?'

'What was what?' asked Tate, clearly annoyed at being told to stop for no good reason.

'That driveway.'

'What driveway?'

'Just back there. We shot past it. Overgrown as hell. Let's check it out!'

'Fucksake, we're not stopping to check out random driveways that catch your eye. You think we're burglars or something?'

Nick swung open his door. 'Well, I'm checking it out. You gonna drive off without me?'

'Fucking should,' Tate muttered, but he, like the rest of us, opened his door. We'd pulled over part-way along a kilometre long straight section of road. By the time Tate had stopped, a bit of distance had been covered, so we had to walk perhaps a hundred metres back up the road. Tate could have simply reversed the car or ripped a u-turn, but he was in a pissy mood and seemed determined to sulk about having to walk.

When we finally arrived at what Nick had seen, I had to admit that it looked intriguing. There had clearly once been a driveway. Where it connected with the road, and for the next few metres, it was beautifully concreted, sloping away at the sides into a drain that ran parallel to the highway. Beyond those several metres though, there was nothing but neglect. Bamboo had been planted on each side, and it had grown in, advancing centimetre by centimetre towards the middle of the erstwhile driveway. There was now no way through for a vehicle. Even for pedestrians, the corridor was narrow, the long green stalks meeting above our heads in a steep arch.

There was no conscious group decision to advance. We simply began shuffling through the archway. The bamboo corridor ran for about thirty metres. It was beautiful in its own weird way, with the dappled afternoon light splashing through as the tall stalks moved in the slight breeze. Then we were out the other side, and we all - each one of us - flat out gasped.

Up ahead, at the end of the driveway, was a sight that had to be seen to be believed. A vast, two-storied house sat there before us. It was grand, the country opulence we'd seen in old American films. Off to the left of the house was a tennis court, its tall wire fence choked by climbing roses that had run rampant for decades. The court itself - as much as we could see - was a mess, weeds sprouting up through the cracked concrete as nature took its toll.

It wasn't just the tennis court. Where the bamboo ended, the driveway was more greenery than gravel. The lawns were a waist-high sea of paspalum, and the gardens had long since gone to ruin.

At first glance, the house seemed to have been spared the degradations suffered by the grounds. However, on closer inspection, we could see that it was also in a terrible state of disrepair. Decades-old paint was flaking, peeling or non-existent. The corrugated iron roof was a sea of rust. An occasional window was shattered, either by nature or human enterprise. The front porch roof slumped and sagged, the result of one of the supports having rotted away and snapped.

Kevin led the way as we pushed through the once-was-driveway towards the front door. We approached the entrance, looking nervously at the collapsing porch. With an 'It hasn't crashed down yet so surely it's good for a few more hours' attitude, we stepped up and Kevin pushed at the door. It swung inward at his touch. The wood around the lock was splintered, and there were dents in the door's surface. Someone must have busted it open at some point.

Kevin peered inside, before stepping forward past the threshold. 'Seems okay.'

We followed him in, Tate bringing up the rear. We were in a large foyer, where hats and coats would have been collected, the empty hooks still lining the walls. Directly ahead, a staircase made its way upwards, while doorways led off to the left and right. The interior was all white painted wood, vertical boards between wide skirtings and architraves. I surveyed the ceiling admiringly. Chunky exposed beams ran the width of the room and patterned plaster boards were intersected by native timber battens.

The effect was spoiled by the tagging. Someone had spray-painted something indecipherable on every available surface. In the middle of the floor, the 'artist' had sprayed a large swastika.

'Pricks,' muttered Nick. He was Maori and had had the snot kicked out of him by a skinhead in Takapuna one evening back in our Auckland days.

We conducted a basic reconnaissance of the ground floor. The tagging continued, the culprits intent on using the entirety of their paint cans. It was an odd place. There was still furniture, for a start. The main pieces had gone, but whoever had vacated the house had left numerous random items. A massive armchair sat in one room; a whole stand-alone sideboard and hutch cabinet stood in what must have been the dining room; and various small tables and large bookshelves decorated other rooms. There was even a piano, its stool placed in front of it, waiting for someone to sit down and bang out another tune. Cobwebs and dust coated most surfaces.

The whole vibe was deeply unsettling. The inescapable conclusion was that the occupant had left in a hurry. My imagination writhed as I considered why that might have been.

'This is nice stuff!' exclaimed Nick, running his fingers down the side of an empty bookshelf. He then rubbed his hands together, dusting off the grime of ages that had coated his fingers. 'Who leaves expensive furniture behind?'

'Run out of town by the gangs?' I asked.

'Nah, doubt it. Any gang worth their shit would have loaded this stuff up and sold it themselves, wouldn't they?'

'Hey lads.' It was Tate. 'Shall I go bring the car closer and grab the beers?'

We all nodded our approval. Tate was in tacit apology mode. Having thrown his toys when Nick forced him to stop, he was now just as intrigued as the rest of us. As Tate left, Nick, Kevin and I dragged various items of furniture into what would have been the lounge - the armchair; a large, low coffee table; the piano stool. We soon had enough serviceable bits and pieces to sit on, and when Tate arrived back, we cracked open a beer each and took our dust-covered seats.

We talked shit for a while as our beer slid down and we finished a second and a third. Then Kevin noted that we hadn't yet checked out the upper floor, so, beers in hand, we trooped up the stairs. It was a wooden staircase, in keeping with the rest of the house. Each step was covered in faded old Axminster carpet, mouse-droppings and insect remains forming strange patterns as we climbed.

As we wandered the upstairs rooms, we encountered a similar situation to the ground floor. Here, a bed; there, a tallboy, the contents of the drawers removed, but the item itself remaining. Tree branches had smashed several windows in one of the back rooms, and a swathe of virulent-looking mould was devouring the grey carpet and patterned wallpaper.

'Bloody hell!' called Kevin from another room, and we rushed to join him. A beautiful leather-topped desk sat against one wall, assorted pens and other stationary lying in plain sight. A record player was placed atop a small waist-high set of shelves packed full of old vinyl. Two metal filing cabinets lurked against another wall, with several bookshelves filling other gaps. The shelves were filled with cardboard or leather spines - books on farming practices; folders with handwritten titles scrawled on their backs; the occasional pulp novel or volume of cartoons that must have appealed to the room's last occupant. Dust coated every surface. If it weren't for the dust, we would have expected to have been surprised at any moment by an irate house owner wondering what we were doing trespassing in his office.

'Sheeit,' whistled Kevin. He'd pulled open several of the filing cabinet drawers. They were packed with papers. 'This is business stuff,' he said, pulling out a sheaf and leafing through them. 'Who leaves this shit behind?'

He was right. The cabinets were full of business records. There were sheep and cattle purchases and sales, productivity records, employment records. The paperwork went back decades, a comprehensive account of a working farm station. Some of it was juicy stuff. Tate found a folder detailing the firing of a farm manager in the sixties. As he read through the catalogue of allegations levelled against the unfortunate manager - drug use, drunkenness, sexual shenanigans, all relayed in grim detail - we were in hysterics. Tate was a funny bugger when he wanted to be, a real comedian when he wasn't throwing hissy fits, and he had me and Nick hanging on his every word.

Which is why we hadn't noticed that Kevin wasn't laughing. He had separated himself from us, and was sitting on a small reading chair next to the desk, a notebook in his hands. 'Daaamn!' he muttered, and we turned to look at him. He waved the notebook at us. It was about the size of an average diary, with a thick leather cover. There was nothing printed on the outside; it was plain, stark black, expensive looking. The inside pages were unlined, covered with painstakingly neat handwriting printed in an uncomplicated, sloping style.

Kevin began to read.

3 September 1977

Anyone who reads this will think this is a hoax. However, I need to put this down in writing before even I begin to believe that I've lost my mind.

Before starting, I should note down some details about myself, for later readers, if any. My name is Frances Reagan and I am sixty-two years old. My wife Phyllis is long since in the grave and our only child, Stephen, died three years ago in a logging accident. I own a large farm here on the East Coast, although the day-to-day running of the place is now handled by a farm manager and several other employees. For all intents and purposes, I appear to have become accidentally retired.

I am writing these words in the upstairs study of my home, which is on the edge of the farm. The study contains my desk, my business records, my favourite books, a record player and my music. It is a largish, square room, with several bookcases and filing cabinets, and a table/shelf for the record player.

We all took our time looking around the room, taking in the objects that were described, still sitting there some one and a half decades on.

I describe the room so it can be envisaged by someone independent, as it is the room where the strange occurrence manifested itself. Forgive my lack of articulation and any deficiencies in my description. I am a farmer, not a writer.

The occurrence became visible at approximately 5.40pm last night. I was sitting at my desk - the same desk at which I am currently seated - when out of the corner of my eye I noticed a most curious sight. The patterns of my wallpaper were moving. They seemed to swim in a strange, eddying motion, like the edge of the sea moving in and around the humps and dips of the beach.

I realise that I have forgotten to describe the wallpaper, which is perhaps the most important part of the room, given this event. It is a somewhat avant garde pattern - a series of what looks like black and white brush-strokes in different directions - that my wife chose when we first renovated the house. Her taste was always ahead of her time.

The brush-strokes were moving, performing an unnatural asymmetric dance, while I watched aghast. You won't be able to comprehend the strangeness of watching wallpaper move. Anyone who reads this will accuse me of imbibing marijuana or something of that ilk, but I can wholeheartedly confirm that nothing could be further from the truth.

I watched the wallpaper patterns move, and, despite my astonishment, I attempted to monitor what I was seeing. It was not the whole wall that was affected, nor were any of the surrounding walls displaying effects out of the ordinary. On the sole wall where the moving patterns exhibited themselves, the effect was limited to what appeared to be a large oval, the elongation occurring along the horizontal axis.

I could discern no obvious repetition in the movements. The swirls and eddies seemed entirely random, motion without meaning.

Then, as abruptly as it had begun, it was gone, and my study wall returned to normal. I sat still for a time, anticipating something further occurring, afraid to approach. I do not know how long I remained seated, statue-like. Five minutes? Fifteen? Longer? At any rate, my study remained as it would ordinarily look, and I eventually hauled myself from my chair and approached the far wall.

It was as if nothing had ever happened. The black and white brush-strokes were as they always had been, utterly unchanged despite the shifting dance I had just watched. Gingerly, I touched my fingers to the wall, tracing the slight indentations I already knew existed. They remained. It was if I had hallucinated the entire experience, though I knew I had not.

That night, I slept poorly. Every groan and creak that a house naturally makes caused me to start awake, reaching for the light-switch.

The next day, being this morning, I made my way into the study again, to see whether anything had altered since the previous evening. It was as it had been, and with relief that I went about my day. With sunlight and chores I began to doubt my recollections of last night. I had that feeling when one checks whether a door is locked - and one may even check more than once - only to be unable to recall in half an hour's time whether it was locked or not.

I would not be writing these words had I not returned to my study this evening. I had been in the room for perhaps two to three minutes, standing and surveying my surroundings, watching for anything out of the ordinary, when the movement on the wall began again. It was the same large oval of movement as before, but the random nature of it lasted only briefly.

As I prepared to back away and leave, many of the swirling lines abruptly hardened into fixed letters. Letters that spelled a word. HELLO.

I got to my feet, wracking my brains as to what to do. Flee or remain? Speech or silence? In the end, I made up my mind to stay and speak. 'Hello,' I said in response.

I waited, but there was no change to the wall. The word remained, as if printed on the wallpaper, while the formless swirl continued as a background within the remainder of the oval.

'My name is Frances,' I said.

Again I waited, but again there was no change.

Then the word faded, disintegrating into the background movement, and the oval itself evaporated, returning the wall and the wallpaper to normal.

I am still writing this during the hour or so since the writing disappeared. I waited for perhaps a quarter of an hour, hoping that something further would happen. It didn't.

And so I began to write, recording the above while it remained fresh in my mind. I will write again in subsequent days should anything further occur.

<u>*4 September*</u>

I don't whether I should talk to someone. Tell them what has happened. It beggars belief.

I travelled into town this morning, to visit the library. I had not expected to find anything within its shelves that would explain what I have seen, and so it proved.

Once home, I completed various chores around the property, before entering my upstairs study at about 4pm. I sat down at my desk and contemplated my next step. Something had tried to communicate with me - that was clear. But what? And why?

As I sat here at my desk, I decided to prepare several signs. Each one was a word or two printed in capitals on a horizontal sheet of blank white paper, the writing done in black marker pen. I wrote my name. I wrote the word HUMAN (along with a rough picture of a man). I wrote words like FRIEND and TALK.

After less than ten minutes, the swirling oval reappeared. (I wrote earlier that it beggars belief, but when I noticed the change in the wallpaper's composition, it was something I almost took with a grain of salt, odd as that may seem. Of course it was back!) Immediately, the same capitalised word as before - HELLO - reappeared. I went through a curious form of show and tell with my homemade signs: reiterating my name; pointing to myself as a human; trying to convey the concept of friendship. I do not know how well I explained that I was not an enemy, but the word on the wall soon changed. FRIEND. Then the oval faded away.

It is now almost 10pm, and the oval has not reappeared tonight.

<u>5 September</u>

I'm frightened and I'm leaving.

For the first time, I am writing from downstairs. When I have finished this entry, I shall return briefly to my study to lay this notebook/diary in a place where it will be found by anyone entering the room.

What occurred that frightened me so was brief, and I shall set it down now. I returned to the study today at about 10.30am, having completed my morning chores. I had resolved to consider further signs to display once the swirling oval reappeared, as I knew it would.

Before I could begin, it had already materialised. This time though there was a different word that solidified amidst the movement. COME, it read. I stared at it, intrigued by this development. Then it was gone, a new word arriving. CLOSER.

I walked towards the wall. And as I approached, the oval suddenly pulsed. This was different to the random movements I was used to. This time, the wall itself bulged outward, a tumour thrusting at the skin that covered it. Suddenly struck by the image of indigestion, I turned and ran. Indigestion requires a stomach and feeding, and what I saw was the hungry wall reaching out for me.

As I sit and write these words, I have too many questions and observations. As the oval first appeared, I did not say a word, let alone 'hello'. Certainly, there is nothing in my study that spells out that word. How then did the oval know the spelling and meaning of 'hello'?

Again, when the oval became visible for the second time, the only words I spoke were to introduce myself - 'My name is Frances'. Then, the following day, I spoke to my signs and nothing else. Yet the oval knew to ask me to 'come closer'.

Who had it been in contact with, and in what situations?

I am no student of physics or other such sciences. Nor am I qualified to answer such questions as whether life exists on other planets or in other dimensions. Nonetheless, I ask myself if it is possible that other life forms exist - either in our universe or a different universe entirely - which can project themselves into our world? Could a fixed wall provide a platform for another dimension to communicate with us, just as we project an image with an OHP? The bit that scares me senseless is that it is not simply communication. The wall bulged. Could it have snared me if I were closer?

I do not intend to find out.

There are other questions. Why did the oval appear so quickly once I entered the study each time? Was it coincidence? Did it reappear when I was not there, only to fade away when it found no one present? Or did it somehow monitor the room, reappearing only when I was there?

I do not want to know.

My intention is to get out. My farm operates without me and I do not doubt it will soon sell once I place it on the market. However, I intend to subdivide before any sale. The house will be split from the rest of the farm. I shall keep the house in my possession and let it rot without occupants. The rates will be paid, but I shall disconnect the power and walk away.

I do not approve of trespassers. However, should any invade this house before it crumbles, this diary shall be left on my desk as a warning. Then I will walk from the room and close the door behind me. A truck will arrive in the next day or so, and I will load what I can and leave forever. This diary will remain, and no one will touch the contents of the study.

Kevin stopped reading. We all looked at each other. 'Where did you pick that up from?' I asked.

'Top of the left hand filing cabinet,' he responded.

'Didn't you just say ol' Frances What's-his-nuts left it on his desk?'

'He wrote this in seventy-seven. It's not exactly weird that someone's moved it since then.'

'Yeah, but-'

'Holy fuck!'

We turned from our brief argument, as Tate turned to run, fell, and scrabbled across the floor as quickly as he could. I turned to the far wall. After Kevin's reading from the diary, it was the obvious place to look.

I couldn't believe it. The patterns on the wallpaper were swirling in an oval surround, just as Kevin had been describing.

There was a thud of flesh and bone against wood. Tate was so torn between his desire to leave and to watch, he had smacked into the door-frame.

Kevin, though. He walked towards the wall as if what he had just read to us had meant nothing.

'Stay the fuck away, man!' Tate screamed, but Kevin kept on walking.

'The dude said it didn't harm him,' he said. 'He chickened out. I wanna see what this thing does.'

Two words flashed up on the wall. *HELLO*, then *CLOSER*.

'See?' said Kevin. 'It's friendly.'

He walked the final few steps to the wall and laid his hands on the moving surface. Then, as we watched in horrified amazement, the walled bulged, just as the diary writer had described. It seemed to envelope Kevin, as if the wall was no longer solid. Where it wrapped around him he was trapped, an insect caught fast in an endlessly swirling web.

As Kevin kicked and screamed and thrashed, the remaining three of us - me, Tate and Nick - stood still, stupefied. An instant later, Kevin was gone, pulled into the oval, out of sight and sound, before the oval itself vanished, leaving just the wallpaper as it had always been.

Tate was the first to react. Screaming his threat raw, he grabbed a large stone paperweight from the top of the desk. He ran to the wall, bashing at the wallpaper so that it and the thin scrim that lay beneath crumbled and gaped. I don't know what he was expecting. Kevin held in place in the wall cavity? At any rate, there was only dust and empty space. Kevin had disappeared.

***

We raised the alarm when we re-entered Gisborne. No one believed us, and accusations of psychedelic drug use followed. When Kevin failed to show up however, we were each questioned exhaustively, though no arrests occurred. Police visited the abandoned house and found no evidence of blood or foul play. Presumably no mysterious oval appeared while they searched. With no leads, they appealed for sightings from anyone who might have seen him. We three survivors remained suspects, but with no dead body and only a crazed, LSD-trip of a story from the last witnesses to see Kevin alive, the case stayed open.

***

95

We each got out of Gisborne. The stares became too much. Before I left town though, I took one final journey to that old house, taking with me a can of gasoline and a packet of matches. I'd done some thinking, about all the graffiti in the lower level of the house, and the complete lack of it upstairs. What had been the immediate reaction of our group as we explored the upper floor and discovered the fully furnished study? We'd stayed. I wondered how many of those vandals had made the trip upstairs and never left?

I thought about the words displayed within the oval, words that must surely have been learned elsewhere, and a concept kept coming to my mind. Bait. The words were a magnet, a temptation. They were a fisherman's lure, and Frances Raegan, and me, Kevin, Tate and Nick, and all the others who had visited that house in the fifteen years it had lain vacant, we were all the intended prey.

The house was almost entirely wooden and it burned beautifully.

TWO OFFERS THEY COULDN'T REFUSE

It was on a business trip to Amsterdam that I met Edgar again. I was working for a London software development company, and was on a three day visit to meet with a client that had its headquarters in the 'Dam. We had a development contract with them and I'd crossed the Channel to hear their views on where they wanted the project to go.

The business side of things only took the afternoon of the day I arrived, but I'd booked several days leave so I could take in the tourist perspective. The infamous coffee shops, Red Light District, Sex Museum and a host of other immoral pleasures were calling. But that was for the next few days. Right now, I was at the hotel bar, lubricating my veins in preparation for a canal cruise around Europe's preeminent City of Sin.

One of the things I'd discovered about Amsterdam was that the locals seemed to have some kind of aversion to pouring large beers. The British pour you out a pint as a matter of course (hell, some pubs in Munich pour you a whole *litre* without blinking), but the de facto Dutch beer always arrived as a mere half-pint. In fact, the name for it – *bierje* – seemed, as far as I could make out, to translate as "small beer". Having eventually made it clear that a full pint was the very *least* they should be serving me each time, I was relaxing with my proper-sized beer when I noticed a familiar face sitting alone at a table in the corner.

It was Edgar, an old friend from university. We barely saw each other these days, but back in the bad old days we'd spent many a booze-fueled night prowling student bars for loose women, generally striking out in tandem.

I picked up my pint and made my way over to his table, noticing with pity the *bierje* sitting before him. He'd been staring down at the table top as I approached, and as I pulled back a chair to sit down, he suddenly jerked his head up to stare at me. There was a strange eagerness in his eyes, which faded immediately as he recognised me. He had been expecting someone else.

'Andrew?' he asked. 'What are *you* doing here?'

I was puzzled by the note of reproach in his voice, as if he were annoyed at my sudden arrival.

'Just business,' I replied. 'Well, business with a bit of holidaying thrown in. What about you?'

He said nothing for several seconds, choosing his words carefully. 'A whimsical visit. Reliving the past. That's all.'

'So what are you up to these days?' I asked, utilising that tired old conversation starter.

'Oh, still with Bricknell and Sons. Same old, same old.'

'Really?' I asked, somewhat puzzled. 'Strange. It's just that I called there about, oh, it must be half a year ago now, I suppose, maybe more, and they said you'd left. Did you have a bit of time away?'

Edgar gave a slight grimace, as though I'd caught him out in something embarrassing. 'Yeah,' he replied. 'I left for a while, but I'm back there now.'

'And how's Judy,' I asked. Judy was his wife; a tall, attractive woman who I'd spent the occasional night fantasising about, back in the days when Edgar and I saw rather more of each other. There was a long pause in the conversation, as Edgar searchingly examined his beer. Shit, I thought, she's left him. This was going to be either embarrassing or emotional.

'Judy's gone,' he finally replied. 'She left about nine months ago.'

We sat there in silence, uncertain of what to say to each other. In such situations, I was never sure of what people wanted me to tell them. Did they want my sympathy? Did they want to hear that I'd never liked the one who'd left and they were better off alone? Or did they simply want to ignore the subject completely and listen to me talk about myself? I chose a mixture of the first and third options. After a perfunctory, 'That's a bugger, mate,' I launched into a short monologue about life in the software industry.

We continued talking nonsense for a while longer over a few more beers – I made sure Edgar got proper pints from then on in – before Edgar suddenly looked me in the eye and said, 'It was here that Judy left me.'

'What, right in this bar?'

I had had more beer than I should have by that stage, so I wasn't at my most tactful. Perhaps there was some wisdom in those *bierje* after all – you had to refill your glass more often, leading to less time for consumption and thus less drunken insensitivity. Edgar didn't seem offended though. One corner of his lips was raised in what might have been a crooked smile as he said, 'No, Andrew, here in Amsterdam.'

'Hey,' I said, 'you don't have to tell me if you don't want to.'

'Come on,' he replied, his eyes shining in the dim light of the bar, 'we're old friends. If I can't tell *you*, who the hell *can* I tell?' He suddenly clicked his fingers and a waitress hurried over to our table. 'Can you sell us a bottle of tequila?' he asked.

'A whole bottle?' asked the waitress, in that cute sing-song accent some Dutch have when they speak in English. 'I'm sorry,' she said, spreading her hands in the universal symbol for *no can do*. 'That is not possible.'

'Indulge us,' said Edgar, in his most persuasive voice. 'We're going to drink it all right here in the bar. And besides, I've got a particularly sad story to tell, which needs a bottle of tequila to go with it.'

The waitress gave the matter some thought and finally agreed. 'But you will have to pay for the bottle as though you bought all the shots in it. It'll be expensive.'

'That's okay,' agreed Edgar, and he sat in silence until the bottle had been brought over, complete with a range of glasses, an ice bucket and the tradition lemon and salt. 'On the rocks, or a shot?' he asked.

'On the rocks,' I replied. 'Let's savour it first. We can start the shots once we're chopped.'

Putting a handful of ice in each glass, Edgar meticulously poured out an equal portion of liquor for each of us. Then, having passed my glass over to me, he began to speak.

'We were in a nice Mexican restaurant-bar, just off of the Leidsestraat, about nine months ago. We'd decided to take a long weekend in Amsterdam – see the Night Watch in the Rijksmuseum, check out the Van Gogh museum, you know, do the whole culture thing. So there we were, having a nice Mexican dinner, when Judy disappears to the Ladies' Room.

'As I'm sitting there, this elderly man suddenly appears at our table and sits down in Judy's seat. I'd seen him looking at her earlier and been quietly amused by the sight of this old gent perving on my wife, but now here he was, butting in on our meal.

'"Hi," I said, half sarcastically. "Can I help you?"

'"We don't have much time till your wife gets back," he says, "but I'd like to quickly put an offer on the table to you."

'"And what's that?" I reply.

'"I'm a rich man," he says, "and I'm running out of interesting ways to spend my money. So I thought I'd run with an old cliché. I'd like to sleep with your wife and I'm prepared to offer the both of you a total of half a million pounds for the privilege of doing so."

'"I'm sorry, what?" I said, unable to believe what I was hearing.

'"One night with your wife, sir, and I will pay the both of you half a million pounds."

'"You're insane," I said, unable to think of anything else to say.

'"Not insane. Just bored," he replied. "But here comes your wife again. Shall I leave? Or will you allow me to stay and put the offer to her?"

'"Look, I don't know..." I muttered weakly.

'Which meant that he stayed.

'As Judy approached, he leaped up, kissed her hand and helped her into her seat. Then, as she sat there, looking mystified by this random show of courtesy from an old man, he grabbed a spare chair from another table and sat down between us.

'"Greetings, my dear," he said to Judy, ignoring me now completely. "We've never met before, but my name is Herman Brooks."

'Jesus!' I exclaimed, interrupting Edgar. '*The* Herman Brooks? You were actually sitting there with Herman Brooks himself?'

Mr Brooks had made a fortune throughout his lifetime as a corporate raider. With no moral compunction surrounding the mass firing of staff, he was famous – or infamous – for his ability to buy a struggling company, savagely streamline it into a profitable entity, before selling it on for a terrifyingly large profit.

Edgar nodded. 'I think we both reacted much like you,' he said. 'Judy and I both looked like stunned mullets. And when he told her of his proposition, she looked more bewildered than ever. When he'd finished speaking, there was absolute silence at the table. Judy just kept looking from me to Brooks and back again to me. She was absolutely gobsmacked.

'Brooks pushed back his chair and got to his feet. "I'll let you talk it over alone," he said. And he walked to the restaurant bar, leaving the two of us to discuss the bombshell.

'"Is he serious?" was the first thing she said.

'"I think so," I replied. "He seems to be."

'"Half a million pounds?"

'"It's a lot of money..."

'I think I'd already decided that it would be okay with me if it was okay with Judy. I was already thinking matter-of-factly about what we could do with the half a million. It was too much money for my mind to walk away from, and hell, it was only for one night. It wasn't as if he were asking to buy her permanently or anything.

'"It'd wipe out our mortgage," I said, "and we'd still have a heap left to spend on ourselves."

'"You wouldn't mind then?" she asked. "I mean, you are my husband and all..."

'"Well, half a million isn't exactly to be sneezed at, is it? And it's just one night."

'"He's so old..."

'I didn't say what I was thinking – that since he was old I wouldn't have to worry about him beating me in the sack or anything.

'It was a surreal conversation we had over the next ten minutes or so; definitely not the sort of conversation you ever imagine having with your wife. I don't remember much of it at all really, apart from looking across at the bar every so often and seeing Herman Brooks staring at us intently every time. He could probably tell by our faces exactly how the conversation was going, because he strolled over to join us only seconds after we'd agreed that Judy'd do it. We'd talked ourselves into agreeing that it wasn't exactly prostitution. We hadn't solicited his attention, and it was just one night, and besides, we were really doing the guy a favour by allowing him a few hours with a beautiful woman...

'Anyway, Brooks arrived back at our table and asked us what we'd decided. So we told him we'd do it, and his face lit up as if he'd heard he'd doubled his fortune. At the time, I'm sure he gave me a beaming grin, but now I look back on it, there was something nasty - something vindictive - in the look he gave me. Maybe I'm imagining it, thanks to the way things turned out. It's hard to say.

'He looked at his watch. "It's ten o'clock," he said to me. "If it's okay with your wife, I'll take her with me now. Then I'll meet you right here again tomorrow morning at ten and I'll have the money for you in cash."

'So off they went, and I don't mind telling you that it was the longest night of my life. I stayed in the Mexican place, propping up the bar till it closed, by which time I was hammered on margaritas and Mexican beer. As I staggered back to our hotel room, all I could think about was that cadaverous old man drooling over my wife's naked body. I didn't sleep a wink all night. I just tossed and turned till the sun came up, wondering what on earth I'd agree to. I was feeling soiled *myself*, and I wasn't even the one who had to spend the night with the man. I could only imagine how Judy was feeling.

'Anyhow, I was back at the Mexican place the moment it opened in the morning. Oddly enough, it did an English breakfast, which you sure as hell don't expect in a Mexican restaurant, so I sat there with my bacon, eggs, sausages and coffee, waiting for Judy and Herman Brooks. They arrived on the stroke of ten, by which stage I'd drowned myself in enough coffee that it's probably affected me permanently. Judy was wearing exactly what she'd been wearing the previous night, while Brooks had on a suit that looked like it had been bought just the day before in Italy. He had a briefcase in each hand, both of which he placed on the table in front of him.

'He immediately excused himself in order to get a coffee of his own, and I was briefly left alone with Judy. "Well, how was it?" I asked flatly.

'"We didn't do anything like that," she replied, in a voice as dull as my own.

'"What?" I asked scornfully. "He paid us half a million quid just to talk to you all night?"

'"That's right," she replied, but Brooks was already returning and she didn't get the chance to say anything more.

'He grabbed the pair of briefcases and handed one to each of us. "£250,000 each," he said. "The combinations are both six one six."

'"You didn't need to split the money into two briefcases," I laughed. "We *are* husband and wife with a joint bank account, you know."

'There was a strange silence, and I suddenly felt nervous. I looked at Judy and found that she wouldn't meet my eyes. And there was Brooks, giving me this subtle stare that said *I know something you don't know*. "I've split the money up," he said, "because I've got another offer to make."

'My gaze switched back between him and Judy, and my nervous feeling intensified. "What's that supposed to mean?" I asked.

'"It means," he said, "that I don't believe in the universal power of love. I've been through two different marriage and both have ended farcically. You probably know that from the tabloids. I don't believe there's any such thing as undying love. All that matters in life is power, money and temporary hormonal urges. Now, as I discussed with your wife last night and this morning, I've got an offer to make her, and the offer is this – in exchange for five million tax-free pounds, your wife walks out of the door of this restaurant and starts life anew. For five million pounds, she agrees never to ever see you again; never to have any contact again in any way."

'Now, you and I have heard silences before, Andrew, but there was suddenly a silence like nothing I had ever encountered. It was as if the whole restaurant had frozen, waiting to hear the outcome. I stared across the table at Judy, but she still refused to even glance at me, and I wondered desperately what was going through her head. Then I ran some quick calculations – five per cent interest on five million pounds equated to an income of £250,000 per year, and that was a conservative, worst-case estimate of what she could get.

'And then I started to imagine what *I'd* do if I were in her shoes. £250,000 a year for the rest of my life? I'd have jumped at it. Hell, with that amount of money, you could have any beautiful girl you wanted.

'So I can't blame her for accepting. I mean, the betrayal was on both sides really. Anyway, she fixed her eyes on Brooks, still ignoring me, and gave a small nod. Brooks pulled a several page document from his inside jacket pocket and slid it across the table to her with a pen placed on top.

'"You know you'll be under surveillance, don't you?" he asked, and she gave another small nod. "And if you ever make contact with him again, you'll forfeit the whole amount, with interest?"

'Another nod.

'And then, with one swift movement, she signed away our lives.

'Brooks suddenly leapt to his feet and the contract disappeared inside his jacket once again. He was now the showman, the ringmaster, puppet master extraordinaire. With an exaggerated look at his watch, he announced loudly, "Time starts now!" Then he took Judy's arm and manoeuvred her towards the restaurant door, handing her one of the briefcases full of money on the way.

'As she walked out the door and down the street, she never looked back, not once. I like to think that it was because looking back would have been too painful, but I don't really know anymore. What I do know is that Brooks was suddenly back at my table, sliding the other briefcase towards me. "Your reward, sir," he said. The combination – six one six – was already entered, and I snapped open the locks to look at the rare sight of £250,000 in cash. It took up surprisingly little space.

'"Thirty pieces of silver used to be the going rate," said Brooks. "Unfortunately, inflation's rather taken over recently."

'I shut the briefcase. "Why?" was all I could think of to say.

'"Because there's nothing more fascinating than other people's lives and emotions," he replied. "Because I'm rich and bored. Because I believe that everything has a price, and I'm prepared to prove it. Take your pick. But remember, you sold her first."

'Then he walked swiftly to the door and was gone. I let him go without a word. I could have yelled at him or grabbed him and hit him or a hundred other things, but I merely sat there in silence at the table, looking down at a briefcase full of money and a cold cup of coffee.

'I read something later, an article about billionaires, that his fortune was so huge that it was statistically impossible for him to spend it before he died, given the profit he'd have been making on his investments. He probably earned more in that twelve hour period than what he spent on us.'

Edgar stopped speaking. His eyes were fixed on some invisible spot on the back wall behind my shoulder.

'So you haven't seen her since?' I asked.

He shook his head. 'I left Bricknell and Sons for a while. Thought I'd blow some of the money and cheer myself up. But it's amazing how quickly £250,000 disappears. You pay off your mortgage, take a few holidays, and suddenly you've got to go back to work. I take the occasional trip here to Amsterdam, just in the hope that I'll catch a glimpse of her walking round, but of course I never do.

'Anyway, I've got to go for a walk and clear my head. You'll have to stay here with the tequila. We promised to drink it all here in the bar, so it's up to you to keep our promise.'

And with that, he shook my hand and disappeared out into the night.

I did indeed keep our solemn undertaking to the barmaid, with the result that I woke up late in the morning to find that Edgar had already checked out. He hadn't said anything about leaving for home the previous night, so I assumed he'd gone to find a hotel where nobody knew him. I guessed there were some quests you just had to do alone.

SELECTED CARDS FROM A DEFENCE LAWYER'S TAROT DECK

0. The Fool

'The detective said nothing bad would happen if I just told the truth.'

It's a common enough occurrence. Then the surprise when the charge is laid, and the summons issued or the bail opposed.

There are variants.

'I thought I could talk my way out of it.'

'I didn't think they had anything, but once we were halfway through and I found they did, it was too late to stop the interview.'

The rule is simple. The police are not your friend. Always ask to speak to your lawyer.

1. The Magician

It all looked so innocuous. Then, like lightning, the vital question no one saw coming. The witness crumbles, credibility in tatters. The Judge nods, though the respect is grudging. The prosecutor grimaces, lips taut.

Enjoy it. It does not happen nearly enough.

6. The Lovers

He is accused of a vicious assault on his former partner. Former? Everyone knows they've been seeing each other regularly, despite his bail conditions forbidding contact with her.

Today is the day of trial. You explain to him how your cross-examination will play out, should she appear. He tells you she won't be turning up. You don't ask how he knows this pertinent detail. Some questions should not be asked.

It turns out he is correct. She doesn't show. The charge is dismissed for want of prosecution, and his bail conditions are no more. They are free to do as they please.

Just wait until the next time, when money is tight, or he's had too much to drink, or he's feeling jealous, or…

There will be a next time.

8. Strength

There was an epigraph carved on a stone on the hill where the last of the Three Hundred died.

'Stranger! To Sparta say, her faithful band

Here lie in death, remembering her command.'

But two hundred and ninety-nine others do not guard this mountain pass with you. You are the sole occupant of the defence table, and the Judge has ruled against you.

Appeal.

The pass has not yet fallen, and you have not yet been completely outflanked.

9. The Hermit

No landline.

The cellphone number you were given is inactive.

You have visited their supposed bail address, but their name brings no looks of comprehension.

They are not at court, and a warrant to arrest is issued.

10. Wheel of Fortune

Closings have been delivered, and the jury have retired.

You keep an eye on the time, second-guessing their thoughts. If they come back within the hour, that's probably a good thing, verdict-wise, unless it isn't. One to four hours, and the client may well be toast, though the jury might still fall in the client's favour. Four hours onward?

Fuck it. It's a fucking lottery.

11. Justice

She is supposedly blind, her scales weighted to neither prosecution nor defence. Do those who draw Lady Justice ever consider the funds and powers available to the State? Justice has never been blind, nor evenly weighted.

12. The Hanged Man

Walter Bolton was the last man executed in New Zealand, found guilty of poisoning his wife with arsenic. Yet arsenic was found in the Bolton farm's water, and traces were also found in Walter and one of his daughters. When Bolton was asked by the Judge whether there was any reason he should not pronounce a death sentence, he replied, 'I plead not guilty, sir.'

13. Death

A vital prosecution witness is now deceased, which should be a time of celebration. Yet a hearsay application has been filed by the Crown and granted by the court. The witness's words shall ring out from beyond the grave. Death is sometimes not the end.

14. Temperance

The causation between alcohol and the alleged offending is indisputable. A box of Cody's Bourbon and Cola, 7%, is rightly described as a court case in a can. She undertakes drug and alcohol counselling and assures you she's done with bourbon.

Next time it will be vodka premixes.

15. The Devil

The Police Summary of Facts describes how he slowly bent her thumb backwards, relishing her screams, until bones broke and tissue tore. He doesn't contest the Police version of events. In fact, he seems to enjoy your retelling.

Most of the clients you act for are normal(ish) people who have done something foolish. It is seldom you encounter someone truly evil.

This man is evil.

16. The Tower

With bail declined, they call you from prison in search of updates.

'What's happening, boss?'

'Nothing's changed since you called me yesterday. And the day before…'

When life passes by so slowly, can you blame them for calling the only person who might pick up the phone?

THE HAIR

Carl woke gradually, sluggishly. It was a Saturday, and the sun was already high in the sky. His tongue felt glued to the interior of his mouth, and he reached down beside his bed to his water bottle. It was empty.

He groaned to himself. Thinking back, there had been innumerable points throughout the night that delicious, cooling aqua vitae had been required in order to stave off the cotton-mouth caused by a thoroughly intemperate intake of alcohol. He tried to swallow the horror away. Unfortunately, his mouth resolutely refused to moisten.

The groan this time was entirely audible. Carl had been hoping to prolong his sleep in. It now looked annoyingly like he would have to rouse himself and shuffle in the direction of the bathroom, where water would flow freely from the tap and sate his utter dehydration.

It had been Carl's birthday the previous evening, and things had started staidly enough. He'd headed to a wine bar near the waterfront directly after work with a couple of colleagues. A few glasses had been consumed, along with some preparatory stomach-lining plates of snacks. No one wanted to fall over too early. Then other friends began to converge. Bottles rather than glasses began to be ordered. Food was in short supply.

Carl had a strange recollection of leaving the wine bar and ending up in the harbour. He had a feeling that what had been meant to be a mass harbour swim had ended up with just him hitting the water.

From there, the evening was a blur. Had he been wearing his clothing when he entered the water? Had further alcohol been consumed following is swim? How the hell had he even made it home?

He hauled himself out of bed. It was not a tidy room that he made his way through. The "clean" clothes that had made their way through the washing machine remained piled beside the bed, slowly mixing with the unwashed. A handkerchief loaded with dry cum lay tossed in a corner, next to a crusted sock that had fulfilled the same function.

As he he made his way groggily to the bathroom, Carl passed his tongue around his mouth, the saliva finally beginning to flow. Yet, despite the slight relief, Carl felt the annoyance of something gummed to the top of his mouth. It felt like a hair. There was nothing sinister about that. Everyone had woken up with a hair, their own or someone else's, plastered to the inside of their mouth.

Carl made his way into the bathroom. The mirror stared back at him. He looked a mess. Bloodshot eyes, shrunken into his skull. Strange discolouration to his cheeks, as if he'd been punched, but not especially hard. He wondered whether he'd walked into something at some point during the previous evening, or whether the mottling was the result of the last few months worth of hard living. Last night had not been an isolated occurrence, by any stretch of the imagination.

Whatever it was that was stuck to the top of his mouth was continuing to annoy him. Leaning in to the mirror, he inserted two fingers into his mouth and scratched around. It dislodged, and he fished it out with his fingers. It *was* a hair, one that was long enough that the end remained hidden, somewhere inside his mouth or throat.

Carl gagged. It was hard not to when you were slowly withdrawing a seemingly endless hair from inside you. He stopped pulling. The hair now protruded approximately twenty centimetres from his mouth. It certainly wasn't one of his own. He kept his hair cropped short, sometimes by dint of scissors in front of the bathroom mirror. In fact, now that he examined it closely, it wasn't even the same colour as his. He was somewhere between brunette and black. The hair emerging from his mouth was white, utterly devoid of pigmentation.

Carl tugged again at the hair. It kept emerging, showing no signs of coming to an end. Even worse, he began to feel a curious sensation in the pit of his stomach, a dragging, rubbing, weightfulness. A terrible feeling occurred to him, curdling in his mind and making him blanche. There was a mass in the base of his stomach, not only unaffected by the acid of his digestive system, but somehow thriving on it; that the hair that his fingers gripped was some form of retrieval line, the length of string to pull in the bottle of cider cooling in the stream.

He gave another tug. By now, he had persuaded himself that he could feel the weight on the other end. Whatever was inside him was bigger than anything that could possibly have slipped down his throat. He recalled those ships in their bottles that had so enthralled him as a child, the fully assembled model that should not have been able to fit through the mouth of the bottle. But that was not the only image of a bottle that passed through his mind. In High School, a friend had grown a frog inside a bottle, the tiny amphibian slowly increasing in size until it could no longer fit through the narrow opening into which it had once been inserted. It was not a pleasant image.

Carl released the hair. It dangled limply from his mouth, drooping down below his chin and moving gently from the motion of the release. He stared at himself in the mirror. There was terror in his eyes as he considered what might be lurking at the base of the hair. If he continued to pull, what on God's earth would he discover?

He considered grabbing a pair of scissors, cutting the hair where it emerged, and swallowing the remainder. But what was worse? Knowing, or not knowing?

His fingers found the end of the hair. Staring grimly into the mirror, he entwined the hair several times around four of his fingers, gaining more of a purchase, leaving his hand secured at about the level of his mouth.

He steeled himself and began to pull…

RIDGIES

The bar, fairly generic, was attached to a hotel that also functioned as a conference centre. The occasion was a property maintenance conference: how to evict a tenant; warning signs to watch for; how to be personable during property inspections. The conference was a two-day affair, covering a full weekend. Frankly, for most of the attendees, the pub was the main focus. It was getting late. Decisions would have to be made as to whether the next morning's sessions would be attended.

At a table in a corner sat four men. They were all dressed in near-identical smart-casual attire, the property maintenance uniform of black trousers and a nondescript business shirt, no tie. The beer had been flowing for some time. Prior to the start of the conference, the group's members had been unknown to each other. Alcohol, however, was the great loosener of tongues and personalities, and the group looked to have settled in until closing time.

One of the group had been holding forth with the news that the last hotel he had stayed at had been haunted. It had been an old, early-1900s home down in Wellington, converted into a hotel in the seventies. Apparently, declared the speaker, a middle-aged settler-era lady walked the grounds, occasionally pottering straight though ground floor walls that had not existed when she had been alive.

'Okay, seriously,' asked another member of the group, a scrawny fellow with an ill-advised Hitler-esque moustache, 'why are there no modern ghosts?'

'Eh?' asked the previous speaker.

'Ghosts! Every time anyone has a ghost story, it's always some dead person from forever-ago - some old lady from the 1800s; some poor guy killed back in World War One. If ghosts are actually a thing, how come no one tells stories about ghosts from the last few decades?'

The third member of the group spoke up. 'I've heard plenty of stories about recently departed family members. Mum dies, turns up a month later to warn the family to get out of the house. Then an earthquake hits that night and family saved: yay for mum! That sort of shit.'

'Meh. They're not proper ghost stories. Your recently departed family member helps you out? That's wishful thinking, not a ghost.'

The final member of the group cleared his throat. He was a squat, broad-shouldered man, disguising a slowly-balding pate by shaving his head. 'I've got one,' he said.

This met with the general approval of the group, and another round was ordered. Once all four members were fully supplied with beer or backup beer, the broad-shouldered man began.

'Back in my hometown,' he said, 'there were two gangs that ruled the streets. One was a biker gang, the Trojans, who controlled the west side of town. They were old school. No Japanese bikes allowed; only British or American. To begin with, there wasn't necessarily anything criminal about them. They were just a bunch of young guys who liked to ride motorbikes; shared interest and all. The problem was that they were the newcomers to town, so the Trojans, riding along with their patches on, encountered some resistance. And if they hadn't had a few hardened ex-Auckland bikers, who'd floated down country and formed the core of the club, well, they might have just been drummed out of town, quick-smart.

'The ones who might have drummed them out were the pre-existing gang, a bunch of street toughs called the Cockroaches, or the Roaches for short. They'd taken the name after one of their number got called "one of society's cockroaches" by a visiting judge. They took it as a curious form of respect, I guess.

'One of the Roaches' founding members was an absolute animal of a man called Heke Whaitiri. The guy was about six foot four tall, hair down to his shoulders, and covered in tattoos. You couldn't miss him. He even had a cock and balls tattooed across his forehead. Not much chance of mistaken identity there.

'Anyway, ol' Whaitiri got stabbed about three or four years before this story occurred, well and truly dead and buried. He'd been driving down the road, just out of town, when he'd come across a member of the Trojans doing some running repairs on his bike. He'd got out of his car, holding a damn machete, and had stepped the Trojan out. The Trojan had no weapons, except the screwdriver he was holding, but he got up close in Whaitiri's face and then he planted that screwdriver in Whaitiri's eye, right into his brain.

'Now the thing you probably don't know about New Zealand street gangs like the Roaches is that the clothes they're wearing when they're first patched are pretty much sacred. They call them "ridgies," short for originals. Basically, you're not allowed to wash them. They wear them over and over again, unwashed, 'till the things begin to fall apart. And even then, they find some similar fabric and try and patch the things from the inside. It's foul.

'So there's Heke Whaitiri, dead as a damned doornail. And when a gangster dies, he's usually buried with his patch. The Roaches' patch was fairly self-explanatory: a cockroach in a circle, holding a knife - 'cause why the hell not? - with the name "Roaches" in big Gothic lettering below. The thing was, Heke Whaitiri didn't get buried with his patch. He was everything to that gang - founding member, President, chief enforcer. They worshipped him. And so they kept everything he'd been wearing when he died. That meant his patch, of course, but he'd also been wearing his ridgies.

'The sick sons of bitches made a shrine to him, back at their gang pad, blood-covered ridgies and all. Clothing, artefacts, even the damn screwdriver that killed him. They had some back room that they set it all up in, and they'd apparently wander in once a week and give thanks to him or some such.

'It was a bad time for the town for the next eight months. The Roaches were out for revenge, and there were brawls in the street, in the pubs. Homes got shot up, and everyone knew things were serious then, because it was an unwritten rule that you don't take business near where the women and children slept.

'In the end, it took a horrendous mistake to quiet things back down. The Roaches put a Molotov cocktail through a window, but they'd got the wrong house. A kid got toasted, burned to shit. You can imagine the reaction. The community was outraged. And when there's community outrage, there's extra pressure for police to step up and be seen to be doing something. There were arrests here, there and everywhere. Not just for the killing of the kid. It was for carrying any sort of weapon. For driving without a current Warrant of Fitness. For any misdemeanour whatsoever. It affected both gangs. For several years, half of both gangs' membership were in jail, which didn't leave much room for reprisals.

'It was about two or three years later that things spiraled back out of control. There'd been the calm. Neither side had wanted too much police attention and, eventually, that attention had subsided. The cops had stopped looking too closely. The antipathy between the gangs, however, hadn't disappeared. They still hated each other. The Roaches still wanted to run the Trojans out of town, and the Trojans would have gladly crushed the Roaches under the wheels of their bikes.

'So when the time came, and one of the Roaches ended up on the wrong side of town with no support and surrounded by Trojans? Well, the dude copped a hell of a beating. And the war was back on.

'The legend has it that several members of the then-leadership of the Roaches gathered in the backroom of the gang pad, before Heke Whaitiri's bloody patch and ridgies, and prayed for their founder's help in battle. They'd given the old fucker sainthood or Godhood. And, as the legend goes, they get up off their knees, and there's Heke Whaitiri standing there in the flesh, all patched up, dressed in the stinking ridgies he'd worn throughout his entire time with the gang, ready to rock'n'roll.

'And rock'n'roll he did. He walked the whole way across town, gang pad to bike club, with a screwdriver in his hand. Whether it was the original screwdriver that had taken him out, who knows? The consensus is firm though - his only weapon was a screwdriver.

'So up he rocks to the outer wall of the Trojans' club house, and the sole sentry gets a screwdriver through the eye. Tit for tat. Karma's a bitch. There's blood everywhere, but the sentry raises the alarm before he falls, and out pour the Trojans. It's carnage. There's only one assailant - some of the Roaches had followed Whaitiri over, but they hung back and let him do his work; probably didn't believe their own eyes until the mayhem started - but the Trojans took it hard. One guy with a screwdriver? Not that hard to take down, you'd think. They hacked at him with knives, they stabbed him with whatever they had, they shot him, and he just kept coming. And all the while, Trojans were falling wherever he went. A screwdriver through the arm. A screwdriver through the chest. There were a fair few screwdrivers through the head.

'And then he left, leaving utter destruction in his wake. The bodies were fuckin' everywhere.

'Normally, the police in those days tried to ignore any gang-on-gang violence that didn't disturb the public, but it was hard to overlook five dead bikers and a whole lot more wounded ones. They secured the scene, and the ambulances bandaged the wounded and took the bodies to the morgue. Of course, they wanted statements, but every eyewitness is saying that a dead man stabbed them. Descriptions of the offender? They're all giving exhaustive detail of Whaitiri's facial tats. Who else has a face matching that description? There was no one else in the police database with a giant cock and balls on their face! So police got nowhere with their investigation. The only suspect was someone who'd already been dead for four years.'

'What are you saying?' asked one of the group of drinkers, throwing back the last of his beer. 'Did he keep coming back and taking out the rest of the bikers?'

'Who knows what might have happened if a few of the Roaches hadn't had loose lips. There were two of them, down at one of the local pubs, boasting to one of their prospects about what had gone down. They were talking loudly, and there was a member of the Trojans sitting in a booth, just out of sight.

'So the Trojan slipped out of the pub and spread the word to the remaining members who could still walk, and they made their way to the Roaches' gang pad. Some of them created a diversion, lobbing Molotov cocktails over the front wall, while others slipped through a side entrance, where a sheet of corrugated iron hadn't been properly nailed tight. They made their way to the back of the pad, while the Roaches were fighting fires and screaming blue murder, smashed a window and made their way into the shrine room. Then they grabbed Whaitiri's stinking patch and ridgies, and made a run for it.

'Back down the road, a good few blocks away, they had a can of petrol waiting. Subtlety was out of the question. They threw down their spoils in the middle of the road, saturated them in fuel, and threw a match from a safe distance. Caused the local roading contractor no end of trouble, fixing the melted section of tarmac.

'Nonetheless, it did the trick. Heke Whaitiri walked once, and once only.'

There was a murmured appreciation for the story as the speaker grabbed his beer and swilled it back. A burst of laughter came from another table - fellow conference-goers - and the four men grimaced in unison. The hilarity of others seemed out of keeping with the group's previously spellbound concentration. It was a jarring lurch back into reality.

The scrawny, mustachioed member of the group stood, preparing to order another round. 'That's a ripper of a yarn, mate. Where'd you hear it?'

The storyteller paused, considering the best way to answer. He seemed unsure what to say, and the group leaned in. The next round remained unordered.

The storyteller made up his mind. He brought his fingers up to the top of his shirt, gripped the top button, and began to undo each button until he could pull open his shirt to reveal the left side of his chest. Over his heart was a tattoo of a motorcyclist wielding a sword. It was a crude job, the sort of body art that was best left hidden. Below the tattoo was a puckered scar.

'Shit! You were a Trojan?'

'Back in my youth, misspent as it was. I was only bloody twenty about the time everything went down, stuck on security detail outside while the older members larked it up indoors. At least I wasn't the poor bastard on sentry duty right out front. Nonetheless, I ended up front and centre when old Whaitiri came marauding.' He tapped the scar with his index finger. 'That's where he stuck me. Skewered me right and proper with that bloody screwdriver. I was in hospital for weeks. One of the lucky ones though - I didn't end up dead.'

He paused, staring off into the middle distance, lost in the pain of departed friends. The three listeners waited, respecting the silence.

'The Trojans fell apart soon after,' he finally said. 'Yes, we'd won a counter-victory, burning Whaitiri's patch and ridgies, but we'd suffered some horrendous casualties. Shit had got too real. The older guys tried to keep it going. They were hard bastards, harder than the rest of us. The younger guys like me? Well, we'd had a damn good glimpse of our own mortality, and we didn't have nearly as much invested in the Trojans as the old boys. I shifted up to the city, and I certainly wasn't the only one. It was a way out without losing too much face. As far as anyone knew, we might have ended up joining the Hells Angels or some such.'

'And did you?'

The storyteller laughed as he re-buttoned his shirt. 'Gods no! I'd joined up with the Trojans as a young hell-raiser, and I'd discovered that life had consequences. After my time in hospital, I'd made the fundamental decision that I didn't want to die at the end of a screwdriver, or indeed any other weapon.'

The scrawny, mustachioed fellow was still standing. 'Hey,' he said, 'I'm just gonna grab that next round, but I've gotta ask - you're absolutely certain it was Heke Whaitiri?'

The storyteller nodded emphatically. 'We had cameras on the front of the clubhouse. They were expensive, especially back in those days. But they caught the whole shit-show on film. We never told police about the cameras. They'd have seized the whole set of tapes, and they'd have seen things we didn't want them to see. When I got out of the hospital, I watched part of the footage. It was Heke Whaitiri all right. He was a unique-looking individual.' The storyteller looked each of his drinking cohorts in the eye, a long, slow connection with all three individuals. 'I saw a dead man walk, and do more than walk.'

The night continued. Many more rounds were drunk, and most of the next day's conference speeches were missed. But that night, there were no more ghost stories.

WICKED STEP-SISTERS

I hear that my step-sister has made quite the success of reinventing herself. She is a princess now, as everybody knows, and will one day, in due course, be queen. That in itself is a transformation most would wonder at, and many a young girl will dream themselves into my step-sister's shoes as they toil away their days and wish for their moments of sleep to last forever.

No, her change in title is not the reinvention that concerns me. I begrudge no one the opportunity to rise through society's ranks. What concerns me are the stories that re-imagine her background, her upbringing, who she is and and how she operates. The people seem to love her. She is one of them, and her so-called tale of adversity carries the heart of the masses. They do not know her like I do. She is to be feared.

The stories are told to me by Thibaut. Ever since I can remember, he has been a faithful servant to my family. Now, he is my eyes and, to a large extent, my ears.

My family were well-to-do, and I was raised with wealth. My father was a trusted adviser to the current king, while my mother came from an equally well-connected family. We were minor nobility, which brought with it the invitations to the grand dinners and the even grander balls. I was fifteen when my father died. He had spent perhaps four months prior to his death coughing up blood and becoming gradually weaker, stricken with a malady that the chirurgeons were at a loss to treat.

My mother remarried quickly. In terms of titles, it did her no favours, though it was vital to maintaining the family fortunes. Her second husband was a successful merchant whose first wife had passed away in childbirth, leaving him to raise his only daughter, Ella, with the help of a governess and various tutors.

On the day of my mother's second marriage, I was eighteen, my sister Charlotte was sixteen, and Ella was fifteen (though just a few months younger than Charlotte). Following the wedding, which was beautiful though restrained, our blended family lived happily for perhaps six months. We three daughters - me, Charlotte and Ella - tried to live a harmonious existence, to please each other, but the realities of life got in the way.

The first occasion on which I remember her terrifying me was when one of my favourite bracelets had gone missing. I accused Ella, though it could well have been Charlotte who had taken it, or any of the servants. I might have even mislaid it myself, for memory plays strange tricks. Nonetheless, Ella was the one I blamed. I remember stalking into her bedroom, telling her to return my bracelet, and her denial. Then her eyes seemed to go blank. She was utterly still, unmoving, as if her soul had departed, leaving nothing but a husk of still-living flesh.

I stared at her, confused and more than a little frightened. Abruptly, she returned to normal. There was direction in her gaze and humanity in the movements of her face. 'I didn't steal your bracelet,' she said, 'and you should go now.'

There was an implicit threat in her tone. Nonetheless, as the elder of the two, I was unprepared to simply walk away and depart the situation. It was an issue of pride, though my initial accusation had likely been unfounded, and I replied, 'Or what?'

Her response was immediate. 'I told you to leave.' And from there, a trio of large rats emerged from a hole in the corner of her room.

They padded steadfastly towards me, and I screamed and ran, slamming her door shut behind me.

I told my mother what had occurred, perhaps downplaying the extent of my accusation, and she looked at me as though I were insane. It was coincidence, I was told. Young girls could not control rodents.

My mother's complacency lasted only another week. I was not present, but I heard from Thibaut that there had been an argument over chores, and that mother's chamber had been instantly invaded by a flock of sparrows, tearing at her clothes and defecating everywhere, before departing with the same speed with which they arrived. My mother was in tears as she restored order, cleaning the floors, washing the dirtied fabrics, and repairing the rips and rents in her clothing.

I do not know what my mother said to Ella's father, if anything. No action was taken, and my step-sister walked the halls of the house with a smug smirk and an air of victory.

For another two years, our lives persisted in a cycle of fear and unspoken enmities. We never knew what would cause Ella to flare up and lose control. A raging argument might cause no reaction. A sideways glance at the wrong moment might result in mice in our hair as we slept, or cockroaches in our shoes, ready to be crushed as we slipped our footwear on. We lived on edge, awaiting reprisals that might or might not eventuate.

Everything changed when Ella's father suddenly sickened and within a month had passed on. Thibaut tells me there are now stories of poison and murder. I do not believe they are true. My mother loved her husband, though his indulgence of his daughter, despite her supernatural war against the household, surely rankled.

At any rate, once Ella's father was in the ground, our lives took a darker turn. I do not pretend that I am not ashamed by what occurred. My mother had been victimised by Ella over an extended period of time, as had I and my sister. I admit that revenged ourselves, though our actions were not taken for reasons only of vengeance.

We banished her to the cellar. It was an experiment. Locked in the bowels of the house, could her powers over birds, animals and insects continue to terrorise us? We slept peacefully. There seemed to be a limited range to her influence.

After several days, we released her, though we returned her to the cellar each night. It was a stand-off and it was an object lesson. Yes, she could call forth her rodents and cockroaches - and she did - but we could bundle her back into the cellar and make her pay.

Months passed, and I will not deny that what occurred made me, on occasion, sick to the stomach, though I do not intend to dredge up too much of that past. It was a war of attrition, as my mother tried to wear her down. As an example, she would scatter a bowl of dried lentils into the fireplace, telling Ella that she would get no dinner unless all the lentils were returned to the bowl. Ella's creatures would oblige. It meant that her attentions could be easily focussed on something that was not us. And every night she would be confined to the basement. Out of sight. Out of mind. And no longer a danger to us.

The lentils in the ashes were our basis for calling her Cinderella - a clumsy play on her name that the stories she is now spreading have embraced.

Cinderella.

The name makes her seem harmless.

And so we come to the Royal Ball. Ella knew about it; how could she not, since my sister Charlotte and I had talked of it so often? It was the high point of every well-bred family's calendar. Yes, there was the opportunity to mix with the Royal Family, which was no small matter. However, it was also common knowledge that the Prince's ongoing status as a single gentleman was a cause of concern to the King and Queen. The palace gossip was that the Prince was to be married off, whether he liked it or not. For any of the Kingdom's single girls - at least, those with an invitation to the Ball - anything was possible.

There are stories circulating everywhere, Thibaut tells me, of what occurred at the Ball and afterward. Some have a basis in fact, others not.

I do not know how Ella escaped from the cellar. It may have been as simple as a stolen spare key (taken by a bird on Ella's orders as she worked?), kept safe amongst her possessions until her moment came.

The city talks of a fairy godmother, who aided Ella in her time of need. Poppycock; and a story likely fueled by Ella herself. Fairy godmothers seem rather more benign to a populace than witchcraft.

Thibaut watched her leave that night. She had stolen one of Charlotte's dresses - which, based on her appearance at the Ball, looked rather better on her than it ever had on Charlotte. As she left the house, the spare carriage from the next door property rolled up the driveway to meet her, the horses - still attached to the shafts - presumably summonsed by Ella's will.

Then, and I shudder as I remember the horror in Thibaut's voice, she bent down, releasing something onto the ground. It was a pair of lizards, and they remained perfectly still as she whispered something to them. I have not thankfully had to witness the sight of two small lizards writhing and stretching and changing form, becoming human-like. Thibaut saw it all, and he tells me that the sight still haunts his dreams. Ella must have had a spare set of our own footmen's uniforms waiting just inside the front door, for she returned there briefly before throwing down the clothes at the lizard/men's feet. They were bemused, requiring her harsh direction as to how to dress. Nonetheless, dress they did, and Ella was on her way.

With the information that only hindsight provides, I can imagine my step-sister sitting alone at night in her solitary cellar, experimenting with her powers. I imagine her marshalling spiders and rats and cockroaches, slowly expanding the range of her command, keeping it secret just how powerful she had become. And I imagine her discovering that she could make creatures alter their form; her trials, night by night, as she broadened the horizon of what she could accomplish.

What better time to make her mark than the night of the Royal Ball? She shone. Though she had no official invitation, she looked as if she should be there, and the guards let her through. Though her father had been wealthy, neither he nor she had mixed in courtly circles, and so she was an unknown, except to me, my mother and Charlotte. We kept quiet, shocked though we were. We knew what Ella was capable of, at least to some degree, and we dared not provoke her amidst the cream of society. Her ruin would have been our ruin.

An unknown always provokes comment, and Ella was soon the talk of the room. It seemed inevitable that the Prince would at some point approach her, and once he did he barely left her side. I cannot lie. She looked transcendent that evening. Her hair, her makeup, her stolen jewellery: simple though they were, they seemed to put the rest of the room to shame.

Then just like that, she was gone, striding from the ballroom, walking swiftly down the grand outdoor steps to her waiting carriage. If I had to hazard a guess as to her early exit, it would be that she was scared of her 'footmen' transforming before she could leave. There is talk of glass slippers on her feet, of her dropping one in her haste, a breadcrumb for a love-struck prince to follow. There was no glass slipper. It is a nonsense, though she did wear her best pair of cloth shoes which had been covered with individually sewn-on crystals. Where she got the crystals from and when she found the time to sew them to her shoes is anyone's guess. Regardless, they certainly looked impressive.

In her rush to depart, she did however leave one of her shoes behind, lost as she entered the carriage. As the carriage rolled away, a guard waved out to her in futility, before noting the small crest that adorned its rear. The Prince soon made enquiries, with the crest leading him straight to our neighbours, and his description of the mysterious girl who had 'borrowed' their carriage led him then to our door.

When he and his retinue arrived, crystal-encrusted shoe in hand, an uneasy stand-off was in progress. We certainly weren't going to be attempting to force Ella back into the cellar. She had caught the eye of a prince and might well now be untouchable.

Ella did not seem surprised when the Prince's footmen knocked at our door, the Prince himself waiting at the rear of the group.

'That's her,' he said,' and the footmen parted. He held up the crystal-clad shoe. 'My lady, I came to return something of yours.'

There then ensued a most catty little ritual. 'Are you certain it is mine?' asked Ella. 'Perhaps it belongs to one of my step-sisters?'

The Prince looked confused, as did myself and Charlotte. We all knew exactly whose shoe it was. Nonetheless, Ella bade first me, then Charlotte, try on the shoe, both of us failing miserably. I knew why she had done it. While her father was still alive, one of Ella's favourite taunts had been the size of our feet. She was always the pretty one - perfect face, perfect figure, perfect feet. Charlotte and I - especially I - were cursed with large, wide feet. Men's feet, Ella liked to call them. Her little game that had so confused the Prince was nothing more than a silly taunt.

I hear tell that both my sister and I sliced off parts of our feet - my heel, and Charlotte's big toe - to fit the shoe and claim the Prince as our own. I can only shake my head at the stupidity of my fellow citizens. A prince not recognising the girl he had danced almost the entire previous evening with? No one noticing the blood gushing from a sliced foot? Please.

As everyone knows, the wedding occurred swiftly. Once it was over, and the crowds had made their way to the ballroom for refreshments, Ella bade us walk with her. We circled the palace gardens. I was on her right, Charlotte her left. We spoke in banalities, and I wondered what the point of it was. I doubted it was forgiveness. Ella had never struck me as the forgiving type.

All of a sudden, I felt something alight on my right shoulder. I started in fright, then calmed myself, turning to look at Ella and Charlotte. Charlotte too had a bird on her shoulder - her left shoulder - and we stared at each other in mutual consternation.

I looked forward again, not wishing to give Ella any indication that I was afraid. It was then that I felt a stabbing, stinging pain in my right eye, and my vision in that eye disappeared. At the same time, Charlotte's scream rang in my ears, and I realised that the birds must have struck with their beaks.

Sobbing, I fell to my knees, screwing shut my remaining eye. I felt Ella's hand grip my chin, yanking my head to the left. Fingers from her free hand pulled apart my eyelids. There on my left shoulder was the bird, while Ella loomed above and around, her hands holding my head fast and my remaining eye open. She looked at me and smiled, saying nothing.

When she first began controlling other creatures, her eyes would go dead, as if she had suddenly left her own body. These days, you would never know anything was different about her as she goes about her work.

I stared into the mad eye of the bird. As I did so, I heard Ella finally speak. 'I will call a chirurgeon at once. A terrible turn of events. Nature can be so cruel.'

The beak lunged forward, and there was only more pain.

These days, I am now entirely dependent on Thibaut. I still have the family home, though debtors are closing in. I had not realised how mother had been running us into the ground. Maintaining a lifestyle without an income to match leads only to the poorhouse.

In the days following the wedding, mother leapt from one of the upper windows of the palace. I have my own views on what might or might not have occurred. Thibaut tells me that Charlotte took her own life a day before mother's death. I do not wish to think of my sister making that decision, but I will not condemn her for it.

Me? I will not go willingly into death. Someone must speak truth about the Kingdom's new princess. Few will hear me, but I will speak regardless. I do not doubt that I will be silenced sooner rather than later. All opposition to whatever she ever wants to do will be silenced. With insects and birds and animals as her eyes and ears, how can anything remain hidden from her? Even humans, those who walk the street beside you, might not be what they seem.

I doubt that our current King and Queen will last long. Then we will have a new King and Queen. I wonder how long it will be before Ella reveals her true colours?

AN AFFINITY TO WATER

Todd was not sure whether to feel relieved or worried. He had a place to stay for the night, with a free meal coming, but there was the more than slim chance that his host was not entirely stable. There was nothing concrete he could point to as proof of madness or instability; it was more a collection of tiny factors, insignificant on their own, which added up to something disturbing in Todd's mind. It was the way in which the man was so delighted to find a native from the United Kingdom to practice his English on, when his English was perfect already. It was the way he openly studied Todd without the least display of embarrassment, pale blue eyes sliding over Todd's young features, tongue gently caressing thin lips each time his subject gazed at the floor in confusion.

It was a dozen such peculiarities. And it was the shower curtain too, for the shower curtain was most definitely disturbing. Most such objects seem to depict quaintly cute underwater scenes upon their cheap plastic. An octopus drifts by with large smiling eyes; fish bubble along, unconcerned by the pursuit of survival; and starfish float past without the need for rocks to stick themselves to.

This curtain did indeed display an underwater tableau, but it was like nothing that Todd had ever seen hung in a bathroom. People were beneath the waves, though their poses were anything but cute or quaint. Instead, every single individual was dying in terrible and inventive ways. A man screamed in pain as he was torn apart by a kraken; a woman was pushed through the sea, impaled upon the point of a giant swordfish; people were being pulled into small caves by enormous eels; others eaten alive by a teeming frenzy of sharks, their blood staining the surrounding water; and at the base of the curtain, a man slowly drowned, his limbs caught fast by a forest of seaweed. There was one incongruous figure of a man merely diving, but on closer inspection there was a look of terror on his face as the miniscule gauge on his oxygen tank showed zero.

Todd stepped from the shower and drew on a fresh set of clothes. It was a welcome sensation to feel water on his travel-weary body, yet several minutes contemplating the curtain had persuaded him that remaining travel-stained might have been better for his mental health. It was a trade-off. As a young Pom exploring Europe out of a backpack, you took whatever warm showers, comfortable beds and dece meals you were given. His host seemed on the eccentric side, but he did own a beautiful house with what was undoubtedly a large, well-stocked pantry.

Leaving the bathroom and making his way to the living room, Todd found his host holding a crystal glass in each hand. One was passed to Todd.

'Smooth Irish whisky,' came the greeting, 'twenty years aged. Scotch is of course more famous, but the Irish *did* make it first. I hope you like a good aged whisky?'

Todd took a swallow, feeling the liquid caress his throat, and replied that he had no problem at all with twenty year old Irish whisky. He held out his right hand, gripping that of his host, and apologised for the fact that he had temporarily misplaced his host's name.

'Martijn van Dantzig,' came the reintroduction. 'And yours, of course, is Todd Butler, as you told me at the Station. Butler… A very English name.'

He took a long draught of whisky, savouring it with his eyes closed. Todd waited. The moment passed, and van Dantzig's eyes snapped open, giving his guest his full attention. 'I hope you don't mind my asking you here to dinner,' he continued, 'but I heard your accent on the train and just had to listen to you talk. You see, here in Holland everyone speaks English, to some degree at least, but they all do so with the most frightful of accents!'

Not for the first time, Todd was struck by his host's perfect English. Apart from pronouncing the Dutch syllables of his own name, van Dantzig displayed not a trace of a Dutch accent. Though Todd had a plumy British accent that had been sealed in place by three years at Oxford, he couldn't help but consider that his host sounded more authentically Oxford-British than himself.

'I like to practice my English,' continued van Dantzig, 'with those who speak it properly. I do so hate to converse with those who massacre the vowels and forget the finer points of English grammar.'

'Your English is beautiful,' replied Todd. 'It far surpasses my meagre Dutch!'

His host chuckled. 'You are too kind,' he said, obviously pleased. 'It has taken a great deal of work to eradicate the Dutch accent from my English. You see, almost all of our vowels are different to some degree from your English vowels. But creating a proper British accent for myself has been, I might say, something of an obsession. And it has been worth the work.

'But on to more amusing matters. I take it you saw my shower curtain in the bathroom? What did you think of it?'

You're insane, thought Todd, but all he said was, 'It's... interesting.'

'We have an obsession with water here in Holland,' explained van Dantzig. 'When twenty-five per cent of your country's below sea level and you're surrounded by water, it's hard not to be obsessed, I suppose. But I try to keep my fixations slightly more interesting than those of the general population. If I must be obsessed with the water, then I prefer to display it in more of an... individual way. It's a personal design, you know – the shower curtain. I had it specially made. Quite a talking point, I find.'

They talked for another half hour, with van Dantzig liberally refilling their glasses. The conversation slid from life in Britain, to water pumps in the province of Zeeland, to the proper use of the word 'thou', and a score of other completely disconnected subjects. Van Dantzig appeared to enjoy conversation for its mere sake. What the subject was seemed of no concern.

Finally it was time for dinner, and Todd was led towards the dining room. 'I must warn you,' said his host, 'the room is decidedly unconventional. You could travel the world and never again see a dining room like this one.'

Todd nodded. He was growing tired of the man's idiosyncrasies. Most people tried to hide their eccentricities from strangers in a vain attempt at normality. Van Dantzig flaunted his, delighting in shocking and disturbing his guest. Entered the dining room though, Todd was thankful for the warning. The sight took him completely by surprise, but at least he had known there was a surprise coming.

The room was largely bare. No art lined the walls, and the only items of furniture were a large wooden table and chairs and an extravagantly sized sideboard. For the focal point of the room was not the furniture, but the immense aquarium that lined one entire wall of the room. It was a work of art. Seaweed waved languidly in a small artificial current that kept the water circulating throughout the tank. A wide variety of brilliantly coloured fish drifted in and around an artificial reef system that had been built at one end, and soft pink starfish had affixed themselves to scattered rocks or the side of the tank.

But the star of the show was the enormous octopus that lurked in the acquarium's centre. It sat upon a high rock, over-looking the rest of the tank's inhabitants with its large, unblinking eyes. A long, suckered tentacle occasionally twitched. It was the lord and master of its domain.

'Beautiful, isn't it?' whispered van Dantzig, his pale eyes gleaming.

Todd gave a start. He had almost forgotten the man was there.

'Although I go through a fortune keeping the tank stocked with tropical fish. He is rather partial to them as snacks between meals. But I can't begrudge him that. When you don't have a son, you have to lavish your love on somebody!'

'So is this part of the water obsession?' asked Todd, taking a step back from the tank.

His host gave a self-mocking bow. 'But of course' came the reply. 'Water is a part of the national psyche. I merely try to express it in my own unique way…'

Of course you do, thought Todd. *Why be like everyone else when you can be a fruitcake all by yourself?*

'But let us eat,' announced van Dantzig, turning and pulling out a chair for Todd.

Two plates were brought to the table by a plump, balding man in a black suit.

'My cook, Jan,' said the host in introduction. 'He cares almost as much for the inhabitants of my aquarium as I do!'

The cook bowed and made his exit as van Dantzig poured two glasses of red wine. 'I hope you enjoy rare steak?' Todd's mouth watered. 'I find it's the only way to fully enjoy it. The marinade is, I hope you'll find, quite heavenly, and Jan has seared the meat just enough to bring out all the flavour. But enough of my talk. I am keeping you from your meal!'

Todd tucked in with gusto, but found it hard to concentrate on the delectable food with the eyes of the octopus constantly at his back. He was not used to the feeling of being watched over dinner, especially when the culprit was not even human.

Finally though, with several glasses of wine in him, Todd found himself becoming quite relaxed, and was even able to turn and gaze at the huge octopus without shuddering.

As he finished his meal, van Dantzig leapt to his feet. 'Before dessert,' he proclaimed, 'I have something more to show you!'

Todd got to his feet and followed his host from the room. They passed through several doors and a short section of corridor, arriving in a completely empty room. Todd looked around in confusion. Constructed out of floor to ceiling brushed concrete, the room seemed entirely out of keeping with the rest of the house.

'We are now,' said van Dantzig, 'behind the aquarium. And that –' He pointed to where Todd was standing by the wall. '– is where the tank will be expanded to should my little pet require further room. But you can see for yourself how it will look.'

His hand tapped a small button on the wall that had been painted to blend in, and a large glass barrier began to rise between him and Todd. So quickly did it move, it had reached the ceiling almost before Todd had realised what was happening.

And then to his horror, two large sprinklers overhead began to function, pouring down water over Todd in a violent deluge. A stream flowed down his face and into his mouth. It was salty. He banged at the glass that separated him from the rest of the room.

'A wasted effort,' called van Dantzig. 'Didn't you see how thick that glass was, Mr Butler?'

Todd heard nothing. He could see van Dantzig's lips move, but no sound penetrated the glass. And all the time, the water rose. The two top sprinklers had been joined by a flow of water from the sides, and they were steadily filling the section of room with terrifying efficiency.

Todd continued to scream and yell and bang on the glass. Half of him expected van Dantzig to at any minute pull a plug and announce that the whole thing was an elaborately planned and hilarious joke. The other half of him stared deep into the man's cold unmoving eyes and knew that no such salvation was coming. For van Dantzig stood motionless, impassively watching the water rise.

After several eternities of frigid horror, the water reached Todd's mouth. He began to tread water and gasp for air. A small, detached part of his mind told him that he was only postponing the inevitable, but animal instinct forced him to swim and kick and bang again and again at the glass wall, refusing to give up hope.

Then, with a terrible lack of urgency, the back of the aquarium began to slide open and a new flood of water poured in as the levels in each part of the tank began to equalise. With wide staring eyes, Todd watched a tentacle appear in the opening, its terrible suckers subtly changing shape as it moved. Todd turned to face van Dantzig, pressing his face against the glass and mouthing a silent plea. And as Todd sensed rather than saw the tentacle move behind him, he watched van Dantzig's expression. For the first time since he entered the room, the man's face had become truly alive.

McGASKILL'S MISTAKE

Many decades ago, the main road in a certain remote area ran in a complicated zigzag. It traced the undulating topography of the hills, rising in a gentle incline, before cresting the hills' peak and making its way back down. The zigzagging nature of the road meant that the horses and carts of the day - and the early automobiles that followed - had to travel a distance perhaps three to four times longer than that followed by the humble crow.

The man in charge of surveying the area was a bewhiskered, Irish fellow by the name of McGaskill. He was a no-nonsense individual whose mind ran in straight lines. Not for him the aimless winding of a gentle incline: McGaskill was a man who saw a mountain to be conquered. Of course, the particular set of slopes to which this story relates could not be even remotely described as mountainous, but there *was* a certain steepness to them. Undeterred, McGaskill went about the task of re-routing the road. He drew up his plans, and hammered in his pegs, and bit by bit a new road was formed. Hugging the side of one of the larger hills, it surged upwards, steep and grand in its unyielding ambition.

From the beginning, the new road was a thorn in the side of those charged with its maintenance. One particular section appeared to have been badly stabilised and almost immediately slumped away. The budget blew out in corrective maintenance, and McGaskill took his bewhiskered countenance to another locale. Over the years, despite the many attempts to remedy the situation, the road continued to slump and crack. As the decades passed, and engineer after engineer failed to rectify the problem, the road became known as McGaskill's Mistake.

One day, the latest chief roading engineer was surveying the latest collapse of the side of the road. As he stood there, idly stroking his chin, he was approached by a local Maori tohunga or priest. 'Your problem,' said the tohunga, 'will not be solved by re-stabilising the damaged area of road. But you knew that. How many decades has this road failed you?'

The engineer nodded. McGaskill's Mistake had been the bane of his, and many an earlier chief engineer's, existence. 'So how do I solve this problem?'

'You need to move the road,' replied the tohunga.

This was not a helpful answer. With readily available money, the engineer would have moved the road in a heartbeat. Unfortunately, money was not readily available. Noting the engineer's expression, the tohunga explained further.

The problem, according to the tohunga, was that the hill contained a buried giant. Once upon a time the giant would have enjoyed an energetic rampage through the countryside. These days it simply wanted to sleep. All creatures dream, and a creature as big as a giant likes to dream long and large. For centuries, it had slumbered away in its hill, a creature from a different time, finding solace in the arms of Hine-nui-te-pō now that its own world and its own people had disappeared into the past. Did it dream of what was happening above? That, according to the tohunga, was the precise problem.

For centuries, the giant's slumber had been peaceful. But in recent decades, the giant had been accosted by a niggling sensation that disturbed its calm. Odd vibrations crept through the ground. Low rumblings of tyres on asphalt permeated the rocks and the soil. The giant would twitch, and near its foot the road's foundations would crumble and slide. When the road had run its zigzag course, the giant had been oblivious. With McGaskill and his Mistake however, the giant's sleep had become almost continually affected by the buzz and hum of the trucks and cars that sped backward and forth.

The tohunga finished speaking. He hadn't expected the engineer to believe him, but he had come prepared. 'Let me prove it to you,' he said. 'Tonight is a full moon. Meet me here at sunset.'

The engineer agreed, though not without a hot wash of embarrassment that he was even contemplating buying into such mumbo jumbo. And when sunset arrived, as the light vanished behind the hills and the world's colour began to wash away, the engineer and the tohunga stood together by the roadside.

'So what happens now?' asked the engineer, gazing up at the hill that loomed above him.

'Now,' replied the tohunga, 'we climb to the top.'

It wasn't an arduous climb, although it was made a little more complex by the fading light. The hill was for the most part bare. There were patches of wiry shrubs, as befitted any good hill, but sheep grazed this area and so grass was the major feature. Although the engineer had brought head torches, the day's clouds seemed to part in expectation, and the light of the full moon rendered the torches almost redundant. The tohunga had brought with him an old, carved walking stick, which helped aid his progress. The engineer required no such aid.

After a half hour clamber, the engineer and the tohunga reached the hill's peak. They stood there for a long moment, regathering their breath and staring down at the slope up which they had just climbed. Below them, the road cut a dark slash around the edge of the hill, the occasional set of lights flashing by as a car made its way past, en route to another destination. Out in the distance, a morepork cried, punching through the sporadic man-made hum from the road.

The tohunga withdrew from his pocket a palm-sized rock. There was a hole through its centre. 'Know what this is?' he asked the engineer.

The engineer wracked his brains, remembering the old fairy stories of his youth. 'A circular stone with a hole through it. It's supposed to help you see things which aren't there, isn't it?'

The tohunga raised an eyebrow. 'Things which aren't there?' he said. 'Oh, they're there all right. But I know what you mean. And the stone must have been rubbed through by nature. Drill a hole yourself and you'll see nothing.'

The tohunga angled the stone so that the light of the full moon shone down through it. As the light passed through the centre of the stone, a most curious phenomenon occurred. Rather than simply illuminating the grass and soil upon which the tohunga and the engineer stood, everything within the shaft of light became translucent, till the engineer could look down deep within the hill's innards. The further down the light penetrated, the wider the shaft of light became.

What he saw took his breath away. Down below - cavernously far below - lay the slumbering body of the giant. It was hard to say whether it was flesh or rock. Perhaps it had always been both. Veins of some quartz-like mineral glittered beneath its skin, rippling as the body stirred, disquieted by the sudden attention of the logging truck that had just roared past, making its way up the road.

The tohunga raised his walking stick. Its carvings seemed to move in the moonlight. The tohunga had explained the significance of the stone to the engineer, but he refrained from discussing the stick. Every tohunga worth their salt knew that one should never explain *everything*. The tohunga slammed down the end of the stick on the grass at his feet. The air seemed to quiver, an anticipatory breeze. And deep down in the hill, still illuminated by the impossible shaft of moonlight, the giant shuddered. Flesh-rock sinews flexed, and the giant's eyes flickered open. Pupil-less, they glittered like opals, an iridescent spray of colour deep within the earth. The earth shuddered, an abrupt jerking motion, and the engineer and the tohunga struggled to stay upright.

'Who calls me?' echoed forth a voice from below. It was a cracked, ragged voice, weary from disuse; yet unutterably low, a rumbling almost too deep for the ear to comprehend. It was a voice of earth and rust and vast, ancient spaces.

If the tohunga was frightened, he didn't show it. 'We have come, oh old one, about the disturbances in the hill around you. My friend may wish to address you further on the subject.'

The giant grunted. 'Your little toys plague my dreams! Disturb me and you reap the consequences. Come no longer with your snivelling.'

'But it's about progress!' cried the engineer. 'We *need* our roads!'

'Not. On. My. Hill. Not where I dream.'

'But the cost of going round!'

Whether the giant understood the concept of roading costs, or even roads themselves, was unclear. Nonetheless, it knew when a lesser organism was disagreeing with it, and it was unimpressed. With a night-shattering roar, the giant hauled its torso upright. The tremors felt when it had twitched in its sleep were nothing compared to what now occurred. The ground heaved high, boulders thrusting upward and exploding from the earth. There was no hope of either the engineer or the tohunga retaining their footing. They tumbled from the hill's peak, crashing and rolling their way downward.

Just above the road, they found shelter behind one of the few large trees. They watched, terrified, as the boulders rained down, obliterating almost anything in their path. The tree took a hammering, but its trunk held firm. The tohunga had somehow kept a grip on the holed stone (although the stick was lost somewhere on the hill's face), and through it he watched as the giant stood erect, framed in the moonlight against the demolished peak of the hill. Then, reaching out its gigantic arms, it hauled the hill back up around it, sinking back down into the rocky depths. The protruding arms continued their work. Then they too were gone.

The dust began to settle. Yet as the hours passed, the ground continued to creak as the interior of the hill shifted into new patterns. The sun came up. The tohunga and the engineer remained rooted to the tree. Though the moonlight had been bright, in the rays of the morning sun they could properly make out the devastation. Around them, the surrounding slopes were a sea of rubble. Grass was an afterthought, hidden by upsurges of rock and topsoil. Mangled shrubs were upended, while full-grown trees had been bludgeoned.

Below them, their respective cars were written off. A boulder resided in the engineer's front seat, while the tohunga's roof had been stoved in from several angles. In any event, driving was never an option. The road was no more: fractured, upended, obliterated. On shaking legs, the engineer and the tohunga began the long walk to the nearest town.

In due course, the engineer reported to the local council on whether the road should be fixed or moved. He recommended, in no uncertain terms, a roading realignment. The funding was secured. And thus it was that six months later, a new road snaked its way back and forth among the surrounding hills, never crossing near the old route once known as McGaskill's Mistake. It was a solid, stable road, and seldom needed maintenance.

Soon after that devastating night, and many months prior to the new road's completion, the tohunga returned home to find that the engineer had bought him a brand new car. It seemed the least the engineer could do. The tohunga also found a new walking stick, one with carvings that seemed to shift in the moonlight, the provenance of which was never explained, for every tohunga worth their salt knew that one should never explain *everything*.

And the two men never discussed the giant again, not even between themselves, and especially never at night beneath a full moon.

A SOCIALIST REVOLUTION IN A BOOKSTORE

It was a bookshop. An actual bookshop - as opposed to those strange hybrid entities that had diversified into stationary and art supplies and movies and children's toys, leaving the books themselves as some awkward remnant of a bygone era. It had a cafe though, its owners realising that this was a day and age in which caffeine was a 24/7 obsession.

It was almost five o'clock, the end of the working day, and the store was almost empty. A pair of baristas lurked behind the coffee counter, one sipping daintily on her umpteenth cappuccino, the other picking at the last savoury scone from the muffin cabinet. Away from the cafe side of the store, a lone staff member lounged behind his counter, while a customer leafed through a book at a nearby display table. The staff member was a lanky individual, of university age. He sported an ill-advised ginger goatee and an equally ill-advised black beret. As the minutes ticked by, his gaze flickered between loathing looks at the solitary customer and desperate glances at the clock on the wall. The hands resolutely refused to speed up.

The customer attempted An Interaction. Turning to the staff member, he waved the book around in the air. It was a re-issue of Ayn Rand's *The Fountainhead*. 'Damned good book this! Great selection you've got here. Read this years ago, then lost it, and I've been meaning to find a new copy ever since.'

The staff member grunted, none too excited. Ayn Rand was not his jam. The noncommittal response caused a frisson of consternation to pass over the customer's face. When one comments on a much-loved book to someone, it is always disconcerting when the love is not reciprocated.

'Well, I suppose you wouldn't have read it, would you?' commented the customer, with more than a trifle of snark.

'Read it?' came the riposte. 'Of course I've read it. Can't say I enjoyed it though.'

'What?' exclaimed the customer. 'But it's…' He trailed off, as the staff member shrugged. 'Well, what did you think of it then?'

'Absolute claptrap. Pseudo-intellectual rubbish. Literature that would appeal only to a semi-literate buffoon with pretensions of academia.'

'What on earth are you insinuating?' asked the customer, raising his voice. The two baristas pointedly looked the other way. If there was no coffee involved, they wanted nothing to do with it.

'Oh, nothing, nothing. It's hardly my place to insinuate.'

'That's exactly what you're doing. You're insinuating that I'm as thick and pretentious as… well…' He trailed off. 'And don't laugh at me because I can't think of a decent metaphor. If I'd had time, I could have thought of a really cutting one!'

'Simile,' came the response.

'I beg your pardon?'

'You were attempting to think of a simile, not metaphor. A simile describes something as being similar to something else. For example, "The customer was as ignorant as a deep sea mollusk with a frontal lobotomy." A metaphor states that something *is* something else, such as, "The staff member was a fleet-footed jungle cat with no comprehension of fear."'

'I don't think I care for your attitude.'

'Your problem, sir, is that you don't think at all. But will you look at the time? The hour has gone, the store is closing, closing, closed, and I must depart.'

This placed the customer in a quandary. Should he simply buy the book before the store closed, or ask to complain to a manager and risk being too late to transact the purchase? A mental struggle ensued. 'Well, I'll… I'll buy this then… regardless of what you think of it.'

'I'm sorry, sir,' replied the staff member. 'That's just not possible.'

'What!?' came the outraged response. 'What do you mean *not possible*?'

'Well, I said the store's closed, didn't I?'

'But I'm here! I'm standing here in the shop knowing what I want to buy! You can't simply tell me you're closed.'

'Yes I can. I just did.'

The customer paused, taking a deep breath. 'But you haven't shut down the till yet. Surely you can easily ring this through for me. See, I've got the cash right here.'

'I could, but I won't.'

'What? You impertinent little devil–'

'It's the principle of the thing.'

'What? What bloody principle?'

'I'm a good bloody socialist, I am,' said the staff member emphatically. 'I'm not going to stand here and let myself be bullied by an ignorant upper-class twat like you. I've got my rights, and I'm damn well standing up for them. Viva la revolution!'

The staff member was no longer lounging. He stood tall and stiff, ramrod straight, as did the customer. Shots had been fired. No longer was this a case of mere impertinence on the part of the staff. As far as the customer was concerned, this had become a full-scale class war.

'Now see here, you goddamn communist–'

'I'm not a communist. I told you, I'm a socialist. *You* might not know the difference, but I bloody well do. And the revolution begins here!'

The customer stared down at the desired book. Despite wanting desperately to put the rude little wannabe revolutionary in his place, that would not help him purchase *The Fountainhead*. 'Look, in the time you've spent arguing with me, you could have just sold me the damn book!'

'Yes, well, about the book – if you'll just hand it back, I'll re-shelve it and I can close the store.'

In a flash, the staff member's hand whipped out, ripping the book away.

'Hey!' protested the customer, exasperated in the extreme. 'You give that back!'

'Ain't gonna happen.'

'Oh, come on! I'll leave the money on the desk and you can ring it through in the morning.'

'Nope.'

'You just listen to me,' roared the customer. 'I've tried to be reasonable, but you're asking for trouble. I want to see your manager, and I want you fired.' He turned, appealing to the two baristas. 'You've seen what this little shit's been putting me through here!'

The baristas' faces were inscrutable. They stared straight through him with utterly blank expressions, relentlessly seeing nothing that might complicate the last few minutes of their working day. A tank could have driven through the wall in front of them and they would barely have moved a muscle.

The staff member had also cast a longing stare toward the baristas, a desperate appeal for solidarity. Revolution had been invoked, and a revolution of one was a revolution not worth mentioning. Yet no comrades sauntered forth to bolster the barricades; no heads were placed above the parapets. In Dickens' *A Tale of Two Cities*, smashed wine barrels had caused the streets to run red, in prelude to the blood. Perhaps coffee was never destined to be the drink of choice of the socialist avenger.

The manager failed to appear, prompting the customer to adopt a new stance. 'Okay, let's sort this out like grownups. How much money is it going to take before you let me have the book?'

'Typical,' sneered the staff member. 'Always about the money, isn't it? Well, here begins the redistribution…'

'Just give me the bloody book!'

'Not happening.'

'Hand it over!'

'Not a chance.'

And there it might have ended. A five o'clock stalemate: no book sale, but no revolution. At that moment though, the staff member made the fateful decision to open *The Fountainhead* and rip out a fistful of pages. It was an escalation that required a response. The customer lunged, but it was an action the staff member had seen coming, and he ducked away, dodging behind a table of books. In an orgy of ridiculousness, one chased the other around and around the table. It was a large square table, laden with a selection of thought-provoking literature (though containing no further copies of *The Fountainhead*). Books flew to the floor as the protagonists' flailing hands and ponderous bodies rained down destruction.

With the games of chase achieving nothing, beyond a floor littered with books, the customer took the next viable step. Launching himself across the table, he crashed through the remaining literature, sending a stack of Salman Rushdie novels plummeting. A grasping hand latched on to the staff member's jumper, and the pair tumbled to the carpet. It was a fight in the grand tradition, a brutal tussle with no holds barred. Blood flowed and flesh was rended. Eyes were blackened, and hair was ripped from scalps in soggy clumps.

Eventually, the staff member stopped moving.

'Ha!' came the cry of victory, a hoarse declaration from the customer's battle-ravaged throat.

There was no response. A look of consternation crossed the customer's face. 'Hello?' he called. He gently slapped his fallen adversary's face, to no avail. A pulse was felt for. None was found, for the customer's reddened, blood-streaked face turned the colour of ash. He swung around towards the baristas, but at some point they had departed to a back room, all the better to maintain their splendid isolation.

With no one in sight, the customer grabbed the staff member in a bear hug, hauling him across the room and trying to seat him back in his chair behind the desk. The lifeless head slumped, lolling, the body barely upright. Hands and arms hung limply at the corpse's side.

An elderly lady suddenly entered the store, the door chime announcing her entrance with a jauntiness that belied the store's atmosphere. The customer leapt away, turning in shock and guilt to face her. 'He's a bloody idiot,' explained the customer. 'Just sits there. You try to talk to him and he just sits there!'

And with that the customer made a swift exit. The elderly lady's eyes followed him out of the store, her eyes drawn by the blood and the ripped fabric of his coat. Then she turned back to the staff member, before approaching and tapping him on the shoulder. 'Hello?' she called, staring in worry at his wounds. The erstwhile staff member slumped sideways, dropping heavily off his chair. The lady began to scream.

The revolution had failed, crushed in its infancy, like so many before it.

IT COMES AT NIGHT

Nev Mulroney was a man not generally given to fear. He lived alone, and had done so for the several decades that had rolled by since his wife had passed away. Living alone was a personal choice. It wasn't that he hadn't had other offers. However, for a long while it had felt as if it would be sacrilegious to replace his dead wife. Then, as that feeling died away, he found he'd simply gotten used to his own company. Someone new in the house would have upset the balance.

For about thirty years, Nev Mulroney had bought and sold car and machinery parts. He'd buy the old cars and random machines - mowers and tractors and graders - and when people needed parts, he'd dismantle whatever was needed to supply the part.

Nev couldn't be said to be an attractive man. Too many decades had marched past for that. Nonetheless, he had never been a heavy drinker or eater, and his tinkering with ageing machinery kept him fit enough that he retained the same wiry physique he'd had all his life. All in all, Nev lived a comfortable, no-frills but stress-free, existence.

He owned an expansive property at the base of a hill, most of which was taken up by slowly rusting metal. Back in the day, when the town still had a meat works and other industry, Nev's business had been a money spinner. These days, as the town ground down, the number of customers coming through the gates in search of spare parts had slowed to a trickle. It wasn't a great concern to Nev. He'd long since paid off his mortgage. As long as he kept up to date with his council rates, and could keep food on the table and the occasional beer in the fridge, he was a happy man.

Nev's property was sited next to the bottom of a steep set of concrete steps. The steps led to the top of a hill, where a housing subdivision was once planned and then canned. The hilltop remained dominated by the old Catholic church which looked down over the township, over the beat up old wooden houses that spread out in one or two block formations from the main road, until the land became pasture.

Between the church and Nev's was a house built much later than Nev's. Given the steepness of the site, it was largely propped up on stills. When it was first built, Nev had been convinced it would slide abruptly down the slope, taking out his own simple home, but innumerable weather events had come and gone, and the house remained intact. Its occupants, however, hadn't. The previous owner had moved out at least a year and a half ago, when he got sick and had to sell up. A mortgagee sale had occurred, but the new buyers never attracted a tenant. Kids had broken in one night, just after the sale, and trashed the place, spray-painting profanities and busting holes in walls. The new owner had shrugged in disgust, deciding to use the place as a tax write-off.

On the other side of the steps, the slope was covered with straggly bush. The land had been bought by an out of town property developer with grand ideas that had come to nothing. The Global Financial Crisis had hit, and developing a precarious-looking hillside had no longer seemed such a cunning plan.

One night, much like any other night, Nev was sitting down for the evening, when he heard a noise out in the yard. He'd chained the gates shut at dusk, so if the noise was that of a person, they were well and truly trespassing. It wouldn't have been the first time. There had been enough people over the years trying to filch a semi-valuable car or machinery part under cover of darkness.

Nev moved to a room with no light and stared out. There were no telltale flashes from a torch or cellphone screen. He kept watching, in case whoever was out there had frozen after stumbling into something and turned off their light. If there was a Mexican standoff occurring, Nev lost. Seeing nothing, he moved back into the previous room and flicked a switch on the wall. A sole floodlight illuminated a portion of the yard. He opened the front door and stepped outside. A shotgun was stored in the house, but it seemed too much of a hassle to grab it. As a responsible gun owner, both the gun and its ammunition were locked away separately. Unlocking the gun safe was a pain in the ass. Besides, he'd never been threatened in his yard before. Light and a human presence had always been more than sufficient to send an intruder packing.

Standing out under the floodlight, Nev couldn't see anything out of the ordinary. The rusting hulks of his stock streamed their shadows out to intersect with other rusting shapes. Nothing stirred. After a time, Nev shrugged and stepped back inside, shutting the door behind him. He presumed he'd heard a dog or some-such. He'd let it wander. All God's creatures needed a place to sleep, and Nev wasn't the sort to begrudge an animal a safe, dry spot for the night. He wandered off to bed and thought no more of it.

The next day, Nev pottered. After a visit from one of the local farmers about an engine part for a Massey Ferguson tractor, he killed a few hours pulling an ageing specimen apart in search of the desired portion of the machine's entrails. The farmer popped back again later in the afternoon, cash in hand, departing satisfied. About two or three years ago, there had been a problem with Nev's phone line and he had never gotten round to getting it fixed. People knew to simply turn up at the gates and try their luck. Phoning ahead wasn't an option.

With no further pressing chores, Nev made a tour of the outer fence. It was a periodic circuit for him. Once or twice, local kids had cut holes in the chain-link mesh as part of their bored, night-time hijinks. The noise from the previous evening had suddenly come to the fore of Nev's mind. If something or someone was getting in, he wanted to know where.

Tour completed, Nev remained none the wiser. The fence looked fine, as did the gates. As fences went, it was a sound specimen, significantly higher than the average person, and topped with barbed wire to boot. Likewise, the gates were tall and sturdy. There was no sneaking through by pulling them ajar. Well, thought Nev, if it was a dog, it must have gotten in during the day, before he locked up. He hoped it had already taken the opportunity to depart while Nev was working, if only because food would be in short supply if it had stuck around.

That night, Nev again shut and locked the gates. He re-heated a frozen lasagne. The television played: some shitty reality TV, followed by a Michael Bay film. It blurred into one with every other Michael Bay film he'd ever watched, and suddenly he was wrenched awake by an almighty racket from outside.

He shot up from his easy chair and rushed for the front door. What he'd heard reminded him of a night back when he was a kid, when he'd dashed outside to the discordant tune of what sounded like the family cat being tortured. The noise had gone on and on, with Nev unable to place it. He had rushed around the darkened backyard, finding nothing, before returning in tears to seek the help of his parents. The cat had been sitting happily under the coffee table the entire time, and his parents explained that a frog from the neighbour's pool had probably met a slow death at the hands of one of the neighbourhood moggies.

Nev was through the front door with barely a thought, taking time only to flick on the outside light as he went. The noise had by now ceased, and Nev scanned the yard for any sign of what had caused it. He pricked his ears. From somewhere close by a couple argued, and from the bush across the way came the call of a morepork, but his own yard was silent. Then, in the outskirts of the beam from the single floodlight, he noticed a small dark pile, something that didn't belong.

He stepped out into the yard, taking in the metal carapaces that stretched out before him. Nothing moved. Keeping a wary eye on his surroundings, Nev gingerly approached the pile. He retched as it came into grim focus. A frog was not to blame for the night's noise. This was definitely a cat. It lay on its side, unmoving. Its stomach was sliced open, entrails spread out on the ground before it.

Nev forced himself to check for signs of life. No living creature should still be alive after what the cat had endured, but he'd seen stranger things happen, when hunting missions with friends resulted in unclean kills that no one was proud of and which were never mentioned again. The cat's throat had been cut, and the animal was bleeding out. 'Cut' was an understatement though. The head was nearly severed, a coup de grâce following the animal's initial evisceration.

Nev Mulroney got to his feet and backed away. His mind raced, safety his sudden paramount concern. Dogs didn't kill like that. They'd go for the neck, and shake and break. To disembowel and almost decapitate? That wasn't like any dog Nev had ever known. He backed back inside, locking the door behind him while he released his gun from its cabinet. He still owned a night scope from his hunting rifle days, which he attached to the shotgun. It was an unwieldy fit, but it worked. He turned off the lights and, through a partially opened window, trained the gun on the cooling corpse outside.

Time passed. It wasn't comfortable, but at least he had a focus.

Eventually, something emerged from behind the blackness of the dead machines that formed his kingdom. It glowed brightly through the scope, and he watched it advance on the body of its former prey. It was about dog-sized, though its shape was odd, as if it had more legs than it should. He fired. It seemed to spring upright into the air in shock before fleeing back into the darkness. Nev couldn't be certain whether he had hit it or not.

He closed the window. Whatever it was, it had gone again. He doubted it would return anytime soon. In his experience, wild animals seldom enjoyed being shot at.

***

Morning came. Sleep had been difficult, but he'd grabbed a few hours. He was old. The elderly needed less sleep. He unlocked the front door and almost automatically turned to where the cat had lain the previous night. It was gone. He grunted to himself and walked across to where it had been. There were remnants of blood and fur, but little else. The corpse had been snatched.

'Son of a bitch,' he muttered.

He checked for blood splatter trails, but found no traces. The shotgun blast had evidently missed. His discomfort grew. What in the hell would do that to a cat?

He unlocked the gates and swung them open. The sun was blazing and there was barely a cloud in the sky. A young girl jogged past, heading up the steps up the hill. She nodded at him as she passed, and his nod in return was an automatic reaction. He'd barely even noticed her. Other thoughts were taking their toll.

Nev walked. The walls had begun closing in, thanks to his late-night vigil. Locking the gates behind him, he made the brief stroll down to the main road. A whistle blew as the local vintage steam train rolled by, carrying a load of grinning tourists. The regional rail network had long since evaporated, with the king hits of privatisation, asset stripping and lack of line maintenance bringing it to its knees. Nonetheless, there was still a line of tracks down the middle of the main street, carrying happy sightseers from the small rail yard at one end of the town out into the countryside for a brief half-hour return journey. Apart from farming, tourism was about all that kept the town running. With the closure of the meat works, the population had plummeted. Without jobs, people had gotten the hell out. These days, the town was a picturesque, if more than a little downtrodden, stop off on the way to somewhere else. There was still money in farming though, and former residents were moving back to retire, seeking somewhere slow and cheap to live, so it wasn't all doom and gloom.

Nev gave a wave to the tourists as they chugged on by. Smoke billowed out behind, hanging in the air like a dissolving shroud. There were a few tourist spots on the main drag - an art gallery that occupied the now-defunct cinema, and a few rail-inspired souvenir shops - and he hoped they'd made a few bucks with the current trainload. He stopped in at the barbers, which wasn't far away. His hair was well past the unkempt phase, as he'd been putting off a trim for some time now. Today had become that day, if for no reason other than he didn't want to be at home.

The barber, another old-timer named John Mason, was a garrulous individual. He could generally rely on Nev to supply a few choice anecdotes during the course of a haircut, but today he was disappointed. Nev sat in near-silence, answering the barber's questions with bland, monosyllabic answers. He might have opened up about his worries of the last two nights, but there were already three other gents lined up awaiting their turn with Mason's clippers. Anything said in such surrounds would be repeated throughout the town within hours. Clean-shaven and neatly spruced, he continued walking.

Several hundred metres down the road, towards the other end of town, was the local tavern. If Nev had been honest with himself, he had known that it opened at ten o'clock. And he'd also known he was going to break his usual rule of not drinking before the end of the working day.

The beer was good. For the first, Nev sat alone at a table in the corner. He was a lager man, and he supped on his pint and rolled the taste around in his mouth as he pondered his thoughts in silence. He ordered a second, though it was still well shy of midday. This time, he didn't take it back to the table.

'Been a while since I've seen you in here.'

The barkeep, Gavin, was as much an old-timer as Mason the barber. Born and bred in the town, he had owned the pub for the last thirty-five years. Later in the day, he'd have help behind the bar from some of the young twenty-somethings who were still around, but at this time of day it was just Gavin.

'Well, sometimes a man feels thirsty, and sometimes he don't.'

'Very true. And some men are thirstier than others.'

An easy silence occurred for a time, before Nev asked, 'You ever encounter a dog that'd kill by slicing open an animal's stomach?'

'You got a problem with a feral?'

'I dunno. All I know is some cat got itself sliced open at mine last night. Guts everywhere. Throat sliced as well.'

'No teeth marks?'

'Couldn't see any, though it *was* late at night. Whatever it was, it came back for the body while I was asleep.'

'Never known a dog to act like that. Grab the neck, then shake till it breaks: that's a dog's usual approach. Or rip out the throat, not that it would look sliced, of course.'

'Yeah, that's pretty much what I thought.'

Gavin looked over at the TV that was playing quietly at the other end of the bar. 'Saw a documentary the other day about Aussie wildlife. Those big bloody birds they've got over there? Hellish big claws apparently. Can slice a man right open, if they want to.'

Nev laughed. 'Pretty sure I haven't seen any giant birds stalking about the yard!'

'Be a great tourist attraction if you did! Really put the town on the map. What about feral bloody kids?'

'Eh?'

'You know, killing the cat? Wouldn't put it past some of the little shits round here to be having some sadistic fun with the local wildlife.'

'Hell of an effort to go to if it was kids. I've looked around and there's no holes in the fence.'

'Buggered if I know then. Hey, you got any washing machine parts over your way? Mine seems to have carked it. Think I need to replace the motor.'

Nev did indeed have a few old washing machines under a lean-to, and business discussions ensued.

It was mid-afternoon by the time Nev returned home. He'd sunk another beer with Gavin, then run some chores. His fridge and pantry had been almost empty of vegetables, and he felt like cooking a stir-fry for dinner. Heat'n'eat meals were all well and good, but sometimes a bit of home cooking was required. He even bought a bottle of red wine to go with it.

As it grew darker, he wondered whether the wine had been such a good idea. He was already tired from the night before, and the wine (though less than half a bottle - a glass while cooking and a glass while eating) was only increasing his urge to retire to bed. Nonetheless, he took out his shotgun, flicked on the solitary floodlight and took a position, the barrel pointing out of a partially opened window into the night. If there was a feral animal lurking about, killing other animals in his yard, he wanted it dead. If it was kids, getting in through a secret entrance and playing sick games, he didn't want them coming back.

It took a few hours, the radio playing quietly beside him. The Radio New Zealand evening show was on. There'd been an interview with a correspondent from India about the most recent cricket scandal, followed by two documentaries - one about the influence of the Velvet Underground on the modern musical world, and, on a complete tangent, one about chaos theory in astrophysics. He'd begun to flag. Astrophysics had never been his strong point.

And then, just when he'd come to believe nothing would occur that night, something stepped into the edge of the light. At first, it was an indistinct shape, a slight movement that caught his eye. Then he managed to focus on it, and it became something more than just a smudge of motion. It seemed about the size of a dog, though it moved in an odd, jerking way. A dog would have had an ease of motion, albeit cautious. Whatever was out there seemed to scuttle.

Nev tensed, peering out into the yard, down the barrel of his shotgun. The creature edged into the light just sufficiently for him to make out its full shape. He sucked in his breath, unable to believe his eyes. Although roughly dog-sized, there was nothing canine about it. On first inspection, it seemed to most resemble a giant praying mantis. It moved on six legs, and its body was jointed in an insectoid fashion. Yet it was covered in hair, distinctly uninsectlike. A torso rose from that strange, jointed body, and the hair gave way to a series of rippling spikes that fanned out around and behind it. Two sets of arm-like appendages protruded out in front, not required for walking.

'Oh, Jesus fucking Christ,' swore Nev, realising that he had spoken only after he had finished.

The creature halted at the sound, twisting its bizarre torso to face him. It had a wide, flat head, a vicious set of mandibles shuddering gently as it contemplated him.

Nev pulled the trigger. The creature reared up, kicking about in either pain or shock as the pellets bit into its body. Nev cracked the gun, ramming in another cartridge. It was too late though. The thing scuttled away from the edge of the light, retreating into the darkness of the rest of the yard.

***

The night took a long time to finish, and Nev Mulroney was awake for every last bit of it. The creature didn't return, but there he was, staring out into the black, cursing the small area covered by his floodlight, eyes moving backwards and forwards for any hint of movement.

Dawn came, and with the chirping of the birds and the first waves of soothing light, he felt able to retire to bed. It may not have been a restful sleep, but it at least lasted a few hours. His dreams were haunted, images that disturbed but went unremembered on waking. Hauling himself up, he draped himself in a dressing gown, grabbed the shotgun and made a tour of the house. Ideas of responsible gun ownership had vanished. Legal requirements to lock away firearm and ammunition could go hang.

It was a solidly built house and Nev had maintained it admirably over the years. Nothing had entered, not that he could make out. Shotgun still in hand, he performed a circuit of the outside of the building. Carefully, he inspected each individual window and door. There were scratches in the paintwork of the wash-house door. They were deep scrapes, like single claws being dragged down the door's exterior. If he hadn't seen what he'd seen the previous night, Nev might have considered them to be a random act of vandalism, the housing equivalent of keying a car. Now though, Nev was thoroughly alarmed. The creature had seemed afraid of the light, and the wash-house area had no outside lighting. Whatever the hell he'd shot at had tried to gain entry.

Nev was a man who respected authority figures. Police were there to be trusted. Politicians generally had society's best interests at heart. Even the taxman was engaged in what must surely be considered a public good, not that Nev's tax payments were particularly large these days. He made his way to the police station. The town was served by just two officers: Sergeant Damien Basquet, who had been in the area for decades but was yet to teach the local populace the correct pronunciation of his surname (Basket? Baskwaa? Baskweet?), and a relatively new constable, who seemed to spend all his time on out of town training courses, whose name no one could recall to save themselves. As usual, Sergeant Basquet was on duty, ill-served by his non-existent deputy. 'Mr Mulroney!'

'Sergeant Damien.' It was always safer to leave his surname out of it.

'What can I do for you?'

Nev hesitated. 'I've got a problem.'

The sergeant nodded. 'That's why you're here. Tell me about it.'

'Do you believe in creatures that don't appear in textbooks?'

'What do you mean, Nev?'

'Last night, I,' Nev paused, biting his lower lip, 'I saw something that didn't appear natural.'

The police officer seemed unperturbed. 'Give me a description.'

'It was dog-sized. But like an insect. A dog-sized, hairy, praying mantis-like insect. It sliced up a cat the other evening. Ripped open its stomach, then damn near decapitated it.'

Sergeant Basquet stared at him with a look that defied categorisation. A long silence ensued. Then Basquet spoke, taking his time in a most delicate fashion. 'Are you keeping well, Nev? It's only I heard you'd been down at the pub the other morning, which seemed uncharacteristic.'

Nev pulled himself upright. 'Are you suggesting I was drunk?'

'I'm just asking, Nev. Not suggesting anything.'

'Hmph.'

'Do you have the body of the cat?'

'It got taken that night.'

'Okay.'

Nev seethed, though he could see where the officer was coming from. He had to concede that in the sergeant's shoes, he'd be staring at himself in the same way.

It was a conversation that was hardly going to resolve itself well. The sergeant was not a man given to metaphysical musings, let alone the contemplation of fantastical creatures. On the other side, Nev Mulroney was not someone who took kindly to insinuations of mental disorder or alcohol abuse. The parting was acrimonious. The sergeant may well have been told to fuck right off, though Nev would never have admitted speaking in such a way to a member of the constabulary.

In a black mood, Nev stalked back across town. En route, he stopped in at the local hardware store. Remembering the creature's reluctance to enter the light, he bought the store's entire collection of plug-in, stand-mounted floodlights, plus sufficient lengths of electrical cable to almost run from one end of town to the other. It emptied his bank account, but that was the least of his concerns. With the store promising to deliver everything within the hour, not quite comprehending the taut urgency in the customer's eyes, Nev made his way home.

Reaching his gates and the steps that led up the hill, Nev cast his gaze skyward. At the top of the hill, lit by the sun, he could see the steeple of the church. Most times he surveyed it, he pictured it ripping the belly out of the sky. Not today. That image was too close to the bone.

He could easily have walked the few more paces to his gates, but instead he cursed and began to climb. He'd never been a churchgoer. Heaven and Hell and all their intricacies were concepts well left to others. Yet there he was, climbing towards a church, options exhausted. It felt galling, making the upward pilgrimage.

Nev reached the top of the steps and stared dubiously at the structure before him. Though it held an exalted position on the hill, looking out over the town, it wasn't a large church. The town population had never been huge, and there were several competing denominations scattered around. The church was a tall, white-painted building, simple but effective. A road passed by its grounds, ensuring that few of its supplicants ever needed to use the steps up the hill. As a settler-built structure, it had been created from whatever was cheap and to hand, with wood being everywhere and easily milled.

The doors were open, as was only right and proper. Though not a believer, Nev subscribed to the view that any church should be available at all times to the public. One never knew when sanctuary might be required.

He entered. The church was devoid of life. There were pews, tapestries, statues, children's paintings. A wooden Jesus stared down balefully from his cross, adorned by his crown of thorns. Sunshine washed in through the stained glass window behind the altar, the brilliant colours lighting the back half of the building. It was peaceful, and Nev was in need of some peace. He began to walk toward the altar, intending to shuffle into a handy pew and just sit, when there came a cough from behind him.

Nev spun around. Behind him stood a youngish man in a black suit. Nev spied the customary 'dog collar' and relaxed. 'Father John Spruill,' said the man, walking swiftly down the centre of the church with his hand outstretched. Nev moved towards him, holding his own hand out in readiness. They shook hands.

'I'm the resident priest here,' Spruill continued. 'Can I be of any assistance? If you're here as a sightseer, feel free to take whatever photographs you like. Just let me know and I'll leave you to it! Of course, always happy to answer any questions you might have.'

'Nev Mulroney. I live at the bottom of the hill. I'm new to this building.'

Father Spruill nodded sagely. 'Ah. Feeling a spiritual awakening? Or merely popping in for a neighbourly hurrah?'

'You seem very young for the job,' commented Nev, avoiding Father Spruill's probings for the moment. 'Is it just you here?'

'Just me,' came the reply. 'Thirty-seven years young, and naught but a wee whippersnapper, I'll admit. Nonetheless, priests seem in short supply these days, so everyone seems happy to have me!'

'I see. Do you believe in demons?'

Father Spruill ceased his patter and stared intently at Nev. 'Well, I'd be in the wrong profession if I didn't. I take it you have a reason for asking that question?'

Nev hesitated. Yes, he'd made his way here under his own steam. He'd climbed the steps and walked through the doors of his own volition. Yet he felt like an interloper, and he was still smarting from his reception at the police station.

'I take it that's a yes,' said Spruill gently. 'I'd love to hear what you have to say.'

So Nev told his story, and the priest did his best not to give the impression he was dealing with a madman. Spruill's reaction was something that Nev had seen coming. Sergeant Basquet's face was still lodged in his mind. 'Look,' he said, 'the thing's turned up two nights in a row, maybe three. All I'm asking is that you come down and have a look. If it doesn't turn up, well, you're free to call me a lunatic.'

'I'll… do my best.' There were numerous subtexts there, among them being the unstated *I want other people to know where I am before I appear anywhere near your property.*

Nev made his way back down the hill. The priest wouldn't be coming. He was on his own.

***

The lights and cables were soon delivered, and he spent the rest of the day setting them up in a ring around the house. When he fired it all up as a test, the building's circuitry blew a fuse - the system was chronically overloaded - and he had to pull an old petrol generator out of a shed to power everything. Thankfully, there was more than enough gas to keep the generator running - as long as he could remain conscious.

Exhaustion was already setting in. He set an alarm for fifteen minutes before sunset, and slumped into his armchair, hoping to grab at least a short sleep before night fell.

Someone shook him awake. Nev panicked, flailing about himself as he came to. His eyes focused, and there was a clerical collar before him. He heaved a huge sigh. It was Father Spruill. The young priest stood there, apologising mightily for having disturbed him. 'Not at all, not at all!' exclaimed Nev, springing from his chair with a burst of energy. 'Thank you for coming! Thank you so much for coming!'

His alarm went off and he quickly silenced it. Sunset was imminent.

'That's a lot of lights,' noted the priest, as Nev made his way outside to fire up the generator.

'It didn't like my floodlight last night. Damn thing stayed on the edge of the light. I figured the more light, the better.'

Jerry cans were set up next to the generator, for easy refuelling, and as the sun vanished the old man and the young priest took up positions at one of the windows. It felt good to have another person in the house. The previous two nights of unease, lack of sleep and downright terror had taken their toll. A man could only live on nervous energy for so long.

As the last of the natural light disappeared, Nev's preparations for the night to come were complete. His shotgun was beside him, a box of cartridges at the ready. A pot of black coffee sat on a nearby table. It looked horrid, but it wasn't there for the taste. The generator chugged away happily, powering the sea of light that fanned out in front of and around the house.

Father Spruill stared out. 'I wonder how it looks from outside?'

Nev chuckled. 'It'll look like a mad old survivalist, waiting for the apocalypse. Not too far from the truth, I reckon!'

'Hmm,' was the only response. The priest had been none too keen on making his way down the hill. Nonetheless, he'd made a few calls and been assured by those in the know that Nev Mulroney was a good bugger, straight as a die. An unsettling fear had grown in the priest's stomach. Spruill still didn't believe the old man - the tale was simply too bizarre for any sane person to take seriously - but the priest knew he wouldn't sleep a wink all night if he didn't head down and keep Mulroney company. If the poor guy was losing his marbles, Father Spruill didn't want him sitting down there all alone, seeing demons.

The lights justified the priest's decision to come. Mulroney most certainly believed in the reality of what he thought he'd seen. And he had a shotgun. The last thing Father Spruill wanted was a deranged, armed man, firing shots off at whoever or whatever approached his half-circle of light. Spruill resolved to approach Sergeant Basquet the next day regarding Mulroney's firearms licence.

'Coffee?' asked Nev.

Spruill shook his head. He'd never handled caffeine well at the best of times, and what was on offer looked strong enough to explode a man's heart. Nev poured himself a mug-full and gingerly took a sip, grimacing mightily. 'Yeah,' he admitted, 'you won't taste shit like this in a cafe. Probably with good reason.'

The two sat in silence for a while, gazing out at the yard, lulled by the companionable chug of the generator.

'You ever had cause to exorcise anything?' asked Nev abruptly.

Spruill gave a short laugh. 'Nope.' It was a common enough question. If you were a priest and Catholic, everyone asked you about exorcisms. Hollywood had a lot to answer for. 'Priesting's pretty sedentary really. Usually.'

'Tonight's an aberration then?'

'You could say that.'

'Well, I hope that nothing happens tonight and I've ended up wasting your time.'

Nev smiled as he finished speaking, but it was a tight smile, lacking in all humour. He was afraid, horribly afraid, even with the gun and the lights and the human company.

'What in the name of…?'

Nev turned to the priest, whose jaw had dropped. He swung his head to where Spruill was looking. All colour drained from his face. The thing was back, prowling with its disjointed insect motion on the outreaches of the fan of lights. It was changed though, terrifyingly so. Where the previous night Nev had estimated it to be the size of an average dog, tonight it was considerably larger, perhaps the size of a small pony.

'What *is* that?' gasped Spruill, unable to comprehend what his eyes were telling him.

The spikes that rippled out from its body looked razor-sharp. With its increase in size, Nev could make out what lurked at the end of each set of its arm-like appendages: a single vicious claw on each of the lower arms (it was easy to see how the cat had died), and a set of crab-like claws attached to each of the upper arms. It was a hellish construct, an ungodly amalgamation of natural designs into a form that was anything *but* natural.

'Do you have a phone?' asked Spruill urgently.

'Nope,' Nev replied, not taking his eyes off the creature in the yard for an instant. 'You got one of those mobile ones? All you young fellows seem to run around with them.'

'Not me.' The priest had always flatly refused to own a mobile phone of any description. It was his point of difference, a retro two fingers to the chaotic world of modernity: a decision he was now ruing with every fibre of his being. 'How long before the lights go out?'

Nev checked his watch. 'They've been running for forty minutes. This old generator's generally good for about six hours on a tank of gas. A new one'd do eight or nine hours, but this one's a hunk o' junk. It'll get us through most of the night though.'

Nev didn't want to think about leaving the safety of the house before dawn, but it would have to be done. There was no way the generator would make it through to morning on a single tank, and the last thing Nev wanted was for the lights to go out. It was a bridge to be crossed when the time arose. He cracked open the shotgun and loaded both barrels, though he had no intention of opening fire just yet. He knew from the previous night that a spray of pellets from this range would achieve nothing other than angering the creature.

It continued to prowl, backward and forth, never quite committing to the full glare of the massed floodlights. 'It's only a matter of time,' muttered Spruill, half under his breath.

'What's that?'

'It's mustering up the courage. It's only a matter of time before it tries to get through.'

Nev nodded grimly. It knew he was there. Maybe it even realised there was now more than one person present. Where it had come from and why it was here was anyone's guess. There was a whole town available to it if it simply left the confines of Nev's yard. Nonetheless, it had taken up residence in the yard, and within that boundary of concrete and wood and wire it had acquired its target. Perhaps it was revenge that was driving it. Nev had shot at it and hurt it. Would it have gone on its way, leaving Nev alone, if he had not pulled the trigger the previous night?

He immediately felt bad for wishing the beast on others, and turned to the priest, who was on his feet. 'Do you have salt?' asked Spruill.

'Sure,' though what good salt would be was a question that Nev had no obvious answer to. 'There's a shaker on the kitchen bench or a bag in the pantry.'

The priest returned, holding a small plastic bag of iodised table salt, which he poured into a bowl. 'Plan C,' he said curtly.

'Plans A and B?'

'The lights and your gun.'

Nev left him to it, keeping his eyes on the prowling figure in the yard. Salt seemed a terrible Plan C. Behind him, Father Spruill began to pray. 'The Blessing of the Father Almighty be upon this Creature of Salt, and let all malignity and hindrance be cast forth hence from, and let all good enter herein, for without thee man cannot live, wherefore I bless thee and invoke thee, that thou mayest aid me.' He stepped forward, joining Nev at the window. 'What's it doing?'

'No change, it's - no, wait a second, what's it...?'

The creature had taken several backward steps into the gloom. Now it scurried forward, launching itself, a six-legged springboard, so that it barrelled into the light, colliding heavily with one of the stands. The stand toppled, crashing into the ground, the bulb it carried shattering on impact. Caught in the glare of the remaining floodlights that surrounded the now-fallen stand, the creature writhed on its side, legs twitching in pain. Then it was upright again, skittering backwards into the sanctuary of the darkness.

Nev and Father Spruill both breathed again in unison. 'Thank god it's stupid,' said Nev, gripping his lower face with his left hand. 'It threw itself at the light. If it realises it can just slip on through *between* them, we've got problems.'

'You got any buckets inside?' asked the priest.

'Buckets?' asked Nev distractedly. 'What the hell you want a bucket for? If you need to throw up, I'll forgive you if you use the corner. Shit, the way that thing came out of nowhere, I might just use that corner first myself.'

'I need something that'll hold a heap of water.' There was a grim desperation in Father Spruill's eyes, the look of a man who had believed certain things, but never Believed. 'Stock pots? Saucepans?'

'Kitchen. Under the sink.' It suddenly dawned on him. 'Holy water? Really?'

'Plan C. What else have we got?'

Nev licked his lips, then chewed on his upper lip. 'It's going to get through the lights,' he admitted. 'It's taken out one, and it'll just keep coming. Then when it gets through,' he hesitated, 'I've got no faith this gun'll stop it. You do whatever you think might work.'

The priest disappeared into the kitchen, returning in short order with a stock pot full of water, followed by several of Nev's largest saucepans, equally as full. He set them up along the wall where they couldn't easily be tripped over. 'You know Psalm 103?'

'Not in the slightest.'

Father Spruill shrugged, resigned but not surprised. 'Bless the Lord, O my soul: and all that is with me, bless His holy name.'

The prayer continued as Nev stared out into the darkness beyond the light. There was movement. The creature seemed to be regathering for another assault. He refrained from saying anything. The priest didn't need any distractions. There was nothing either of them could do to prevent what was occurring.

'Bless ye the Lord, all ye his hosts; ye ministers of his that do his pleasure. Bless the Lord, all his works in all places of His dominion. Bless the Lord, O my soul.'

The creature exploded out of the night, chancing the pain of the light and careening into the stand next to the one that had already toppled. The second stand fell, though it landed such that the bulb remained intact, glaring out at the ground. The creature kicked itself back to its feet, chittering out of the way of the fallen beam. Which took it into the darkness that lay between the house and the artificial ring of daylight that had held it back.

'Oh shit,' Nev swore. 'Oh shit oh shit oh shit oh shit.'

Father Spruill had been distributing salt between vessels of water. 'What?' he asked. His eyes widened as he watched Nev bring the shotgun to his shoulder. Then he turned back to his water, beginning a new prayer. 'God's creature, water, I cast out the demon from you in the name of God the Father almighty, in the name of Jesus Christ, His son, Our Lord, and in the power of the Holy Spirit.'

He kept speaking as the shotgun fired, then fired again.

Nev watched the creature stumble, then rise, stumble again, and regain its feet. He broke open the shotgun, swearing fervently to himself as he reloaded as quickly as his hands allowed.

Father Spruill spoke even faster, not seeing, but sensing, the closing desperation. 'In awe and humility,' he gabbled, 'we beg you, Lord, to regard with favour this creature thing of salt and water, to let the light of your kindness shine on it, and to hallow it with the dew of your mercy, so that wherever it is sprinkled and your holy name is invoked, every assault of the unclean spirit may be baffled, and all dread of the serpent's venom be cast out.'

Outside, the creature skittered forward, its head, atop its elongated neck, staring at Nev through the partially open window. Its eyes were cold, alien. Its body though showed its emotions. It was twitching, reaching toward him hungrily.

'To us who entreat your mercy, grant that the Holy Spirit may be with us wherever we may be, through Christ our Lord. Amen.'

Nev cracked the shotgun closed, loosing the first shot straight towards the creature's head. It screeched, staggering backward, then straightened, advancing again. It bore no visible signs of injury. Nev reached forward, grabbing the window and pulling it shut. It was a futile gesture. The creature tensed, ready to spring, and Nev threw himself backwards, knowing what was coming.

Glass shattered as the creature lurched through it, its myriad legs struggling for purchase. It cleared the window, as Nev desperately attempted to crab-walk away in terror. Father Spruill reached for him, intending to drag him to the side, but the creature was fast, absurdly fast. One of its arms whipped out, the claw that protruded from it slicing the priest's chest open as it batted him away. Spruill felt ribs breaking and cartilage tearing as he fell.

Nev lay on his back, looking up at the monster that loomed over him. He tried to back-pedal, to no avail. The creature merely scuttled unhurriedly forward, its claws and mandibles moving with an eerie synchronicity. With just one hope remaining, Nev hauled his shotgun high. He pulled the trigger, loosing his final shot. The creature rose on its hindmost set of legs, kicking up at the ceiling, keening and wailing, but when it crashed back down there was no visible damage.

Those flat, dead eyes stared down at him. Whatever pain it felt did not translate to that that expressionless insect face. Nev struck out with the shotgun, swinging it towards the creature's head. More futility, and he knew it. The creature batted the weapon away, knocking it to the side before grasping it with one claw and wrenching it from Nev's hands.

As the shotgun flew through the air, landing against the wall, Nev tried to crawl away. The creature's attention may have been diverted, but it was only momentary. A claw swung down from above, skewering into his shoulder and hammering his upper body back against the floorboards.

It was the end. The coup de grâce was coming. As the mandibles chittered above him, one claw kept him pinned against the floor while the talon that had speared him was withdrawn from his shoulder. The creature reared up again, not in pain, but in anticipation. Its claws were raised, ready to rip him apart when they landed.

Then, abruptly, incomprehensibly, it *was* in pain, screeching and burning as liquid fell around and over it. That insect head swung to the side, searching for its assailant, and there stood Father Spruill. He was a nightmare in motion, shirt drenched in blood, face white with pain and weakness. In his hand he held an empty saucepan, its contents flung across the monster's back as a final do or die.

The saucepan disappeared, hefted to the side, as the priest bent and grasped the stockpot, full of water and salt. He gasped in agony as he hoisted it, his slashed and battered ribs screaming inside him. The creature had now turned fully towards him, not understanding what had occurred, but knowing who its attacker was. Its torso still blazed where the water had landed, flames dancing, crackling. As it scuttled the short distance to the priest, its claws swinging murderously, Spruill let the stock pot fly, directly into the creature's face. The metal pot tumbled to the ground. A claw sliced the priest a second time, sending him lurching back into the wall, a further brutal slice ripping apart shirt and flesh.

Nonetheless, his final throw had landed true. The creature was blinded, its head aflame. It spun and sliced and wheeled, flames dripping from every part of its body. Nev scurried backwards, desperately trying to stay out of reach of the flailing appendages. Skirting the walls, he made his way to Father Spruill. The priest was on his back on the ground, blood everywhere. The beast rammed the far wall, getting a claw stuck in the stud behind the plasterboard, and struggling to free itself. As it writhed, still burning, Nev poured his energy into hauling the priest to his feet, biting his lip till it bled as fought the pain in his shoulder.

Manhandling Spruill towards the front door, Nev looked back. The creature blazed bright. It hurled itself this way and that, unable to see a thing, a pit of flickering flame where its head had once been housed. Droplets of liquid fire dripped from it, spattering onto the floorboards and walls. Most fizzled out, but where enough fell small fires took hold. As Nev and Father Spruill made their staggered, agonised exit, Nev turned one final time and watched his house go up in smoke. Together, they collapsed against the locked front gates. In the distance, sirens wailed, and the lights of the incoming police cars and firetrucks split the night. As the flames roared and the roof of the building collapsed, nothing escaped.

***

The aftermath of the fire was chaos. The local hospital had closed down decades ago, so a helicopter was urgently summoned to transport the two wounded men out of town. And as the final embers of what had once been Nev Mulroney's home were laid to rest by the hoses and water cannons, the investigation began as to the cause. For obvious reasons, police and the insurance company were extremely interested in what had caused both the fire and Nev and Father Spruill's injuries. Was it arson? And if so, who, and why? Had

Mulroney and Spruill been attacked by an unknown assailant who had then caused the blaze? Or had the "victims" had a falling out, injuring each other, with one or the other starting the fire either accidentally or on purpose?

From their hospital beds, both Nev and Father Spruill had independently decided to refrain from making any statements until they had both had a chance to converse with each other. Police and the assigned Loss Adjuster repeatedly slunk away in the face of protestations of grievous injury and ongoing symptoms of shock. Nev, fewer injuries by far, was the first to vacate his bed. He trooped down the corridor, shoulder bandaged to the hilt. The sterility of the surroundings was jarring. Plain white had never been his thing. To be encased by it on all sides was something he could not get used to. He mourned for his old, dead house, with its clutter and resonance and natural wood.

Father Spruill was waiting. Terrible did not even begin to describe his pallor and general state. His torso was a mass of bandages. Damaged ribs meant that even breathing was torturous, and the pain most definitely showed on the young priest's face. Nev had often heard people describe as grey. It wasn't a shade that Nev had ever seen in a person's face. Spruill however was grey.

Nev sat down gingerly. Jarring motions seemed to have a propensity for travelling upward to his shoulder. He and Spruill exchanged pleasantries, such as they were. After what they had been through together, any idle chitchat was swift.

'What do we say?'

'They won't believe us, will they?' asked Spruill.

'Basquet the cop sure didn't believe me. Bet you didn't either, till that damn thing turned up?'

Spruill tried to shrug with as little movement as possible. 'True.'

'Well, you're a priest, so I don't know what your policy is on talking bollocks, but I kind of figure it would be best if what we saw wasn't mentioned.'

'You might be right. So what about our injuries?'

'We can't remember. Shock? Falling furniture?'

'The less said the better?'

'We remember helping each other out of the building, and that's it.'

And thus it was.

The fire service couldn't identify a definitive cause of the blaze. With a catholic priest as one of the victims, Nev's insurance company wasn't keen to be casting aspersions. They paid out. And with the only two eye witnesses in shock and remembering little, police closed their case. Nev Mulroney's comments to Sergeant Basquet on the day of the fire may have been strange, but they certainly didn't help police reach an evidential threshold for arson.

Within a year, the yard looked very different. A suggestion had been made that if the area were cleared of mechanical detritus, it could be subdivided, with two additional houses built. The local economy seemed to be picking up, and a developer was interested. Nev was happy to oblige. He didn't think sleep would ever come easy if he lived in that spot again. The subdivision went through, and Nev found himself with money. He bought a vacant section up the top of the hill, near to the church, and constructed his new home. It was nothing grand - Nev had never been one for luxuries - but students of the aesthetic may have noticed a certain fortress-like feel to the structure. Only its owner and Father Spruill would have understood the significance.

Once healed, Father Spruill found himself with a new sense of purpose. He had been tested and had survived. He wrote a confidential report for his superiors in the Church, verified by Nev Mulroney, and the priest's stock was suddenly sky-high. Though his small-town congregation and his church on the hill remained his pride and joy, he gained a reputation as a troubleshooter. Open-minded and practical, he was often paid by Those On High to travel, even overseas, to resolve problems, both practical and metaphysical.

And his church was possibly the only church in existence that always kept an industrial quantity of holy water on tap. Most normal citizens would have encountered some probing questions had they approached a church in search of holy water. Nev Mulroney never encountered that problem for the rest of his life. It may have been paranoia, but both Nev and Father Spruill spent their lives in constant expectation of something similar to what they had faced and destroyed.

They had been marked. They knew with absolute certainty that there were things that lurked beyond the darkness, terrifying things, things that only came at night.

THE LAST ROMANTIC

"There is a pleasure in the pathless woods;
There is a rapture on the lonely shore;
There is society, where none intrudes,
By the deep sea, and music in its roars:
I love not man the less, but Nature more…"

- Lord Byron, from Childe Harold's Pilgrimage

When Simeon Coppell's father died, the financial world watched and waited to see what the twenty-two year old heir would do. Mr Coppell Senior had been a business titan. His net worth numbered in the billions of dollars, with a portfolio of interests including some of the biggest names in the energy and technology sectors. On his death, his son had become one of the world's ten richest people.

The son was an unknown quantity. Though he had just inherited the entirety of his father's fortune, he had never run a company, nor even held a senior position in any of his father's numerous business entities. What did he believe in? Was he a risk-taker or a financial conservative? Would he be a hands on leader or a silent observer, leaving a board of seasoned managers to get on with their jobs?

His business and managerial acumen was not the only unknown. So too was his personal life. Though his face occasionally graced the inside pages of various women's and teen magazines, there had been no dalliances with famous models or socialites. No rumours had swirled, nor gossip done the rounds. Simeon Coppell was a mystery.

***

Sell.

The order caused conniptions amongst financial reporters the world over. The Coppell empire was to be disbanded, cashed up. Young Simeon appeared to have no interest in walking in his father's shoes.

The speculators swooped. Selling off billions of dollars in shares was bound to cause a drop in market price, and so it proved. By the time the final shares were sold, hundreds of millions of dollars had been wiped off the young heir's bottom line. He retained a stake in just two companies: a small, loss-making operation investigating nuclear decay as a means of powering long-life batteries, and an equally small, equally loss-making enterprise devoted to atmospheric testing equipment. The market analysts shook their collective heads and wrote sage opinion pieces concerning the folly of Coppell Senior's son and heir.

Simeon Coppell was of course still a billionaire many times over. He had merely become a young, single, cashed up multi-billionaire. The models and socialites swarmed, without success.

In time, Coppell's first new venture was unveiled to the world. Cryogenics. As others sought to send private citizens to the moon, Mars and beyond, Simeon Coppell offered investors the opportunity to sleep through the whole palaver. 'Wake me up once we're there' became the company tag-line. The financial analysts scratched their chins. It seemed an odd enterprise, if the goal was to make money. There were already other minor companies offering a similar product, generally to those suffering terminal illness. The consensus was that

Simeon Coppell had lost his mind. The customer base was too small. Government subsidies would be out of the question, given the industry was effectively about taking people *out* of the labour and investment markets. The project was a gigantic loss waiting to happen.

***

Years slid past. The atmospheric testing equipment company proved a moderate success; the nuclear battery company rather less so. Not that the batteries didn't work. They were in fact eminently successful. The issue was their cost. Why pay tens of thousands for a battery that would last for hundreds of years, when you could buy something for a fraction of the price that would still last for tens of years?

The cryogenics company had never made a profit either. Hundreds of millions of dollars had been spent creating a state-of-the-art facility in central USA. It was bomb-proof, flood-proof, earthquake-proof, and, as far as was humanly possible, idiot-proof. The customers though were few. The place was a monetary sinkhole.

Nonetheless, Simeon Coppell's grand plan finally came to fruition. With his fortune placed in a multitude of trusts, he announced his intention to be cryogenically frozen. His batteries could power the facility for lifetime after lifetime. The earth could shake, and the climate could change, but his building, with its human cargo, would remain.

Simeon Coppell was twenty-nine when he entered the chamber that would house him until his next life. Other customers set time-frames to their reawakenings - a hundred years; two hundred; any arbitrary number. Simeon set no date.

***

Cities burned. Vast swathes of land flooded. Governments fell and rose and fell again. But Simeon Coppell had never been interested in the workings of humankind. Above the earth, his satellites continued their communication with his machine-run complex, and the building's information-gathering functions fed data into the facility's core. As civilisation folded, his computer systems, antiquated though they were by then, continued to record it all.

***

The day came when Simeon awoke. A certain set of preconditions had been fulfilled. His machines performed their functions as programmed, and he stepped forward into an expanse of metal and plastic. It took some time for him to negotiate the building's changes, to bring up the data that described the present environmental situation, and to understand the advances in the facility itself.

His programmes had worked perfectly. The atmosphere outside was stable and breathable, healthier than when he had gone into stasis. Inside, the facility was long since abandoned. Simeon Coppell was alone.

He made his through the building's many floors. There were empty capsules everywhere. Whatever their occupants had sought, they had lived again and died long before Simeon's rebirth. Not all the capsules were empty though, and Simeon moved from one to the next. Overrides existed, known only to himself. He utilised them, ending forever those who had slept within.

Outside, Simeon found a world untamed. Where once a featureless desert had sprawled for kilometre after kilometre, a forest now spread out before him, extending in all directions. Everything was greenery and birdsong. He could not be sure when another human had last stepped foot in these parts, or even if other humans still survived.

He reentered the structure from which he had come. Deep inside the bowels of the building was an airtight safe, still locked, as per his instructions. He opened it. With a hissing rush, air flooded into the previously sterile space. The contents of the safe had been stored in as close to a vacuum as possible. What lay within was perfectly preserved - a stack of leather-bound notebooks and graphite pencils.

Taking up one of each, Simeon returned to the outside world. Amidst the solitude of an earth with no governments or cities or industry, he sat down in the lush grass and began to write.

The last Romantic Poet.

ABOUT THE AUTHOR

Jonathan Natusch is, for his sins, a criminal and family lawyer (in that he practises both criminal law and family law, as opposed to being a family lawyer who is also a criminal). He lives in Gisborne, New Zealand, with his cat, and four chickens.

Since he was very young, he's loved books. These days, he openly acknowledges that he's a book fetishist.

When he's not reading, practising law, gardening, or destroying his gangly body on a soccer field, he tries to find time to write. This is his first collection of short stories.

Jonathan can be found on Twitter @jononatusch and can be contacted by email at jgnatusch@gmail.com